How to Win a DUKE'S HEART

SEDUCTIVE SCOUNDRELS

COLLETTE CAMERON

Blue Rose Romance®
Portland, Oregon

Sweet-to-Spicy Timeless Romance®

HOW TO WIN A DUKE'S HEART
Seductive Scoundrels
Copyright © 2021 Collette Cameron®
Cover Art: Kim Killion

Attn: Permissions Coordinator
Blue Rose Romance®
8420 N Ivanhoe # 83054
Portland, Oregon 97203

Print Book ISBN: 9781955259118

collettecameron.com

"Which is it, lass?
This aggravatin' thing,
this perplexin' spark between us?
Love or war?"

Seductive Scoundrels

A Diamond for a Duke

Only a Duke Would Dare

A December with a Duke

What Would a Duke Do?

Wooed by a Wicked Duke

Duchess of His Heart

Never Dance with a Duke

Earl of Wainthorpe

Earl of Scarborough

Wedding her Christmas Duke

The Debutante and the Duke

Earl of Keyworth

Loved by a Dangerous Duke

How to Win a Duke's Heart

When a Duke Desires a Lass – *Coming soon!*

Check out Collette's Other Series

Daughters of Desire (Scandalous Ladies)

Highland Heather Romancing a Scot

The Blue Rose Regency Romances:
The Culpepper Misses

Castle Brides

The Honorable Rogues®

Heart of a Scot

Collections

Lords in Love

The Honorable Rogues® Books 1-3

The Honorable Rogues® Books 4-6

Seductive Scoundrels Series Books 1-3

Seductive Scoundrels Series Books 4-6

The Blue Rose Regency Romances:
The Culpepper Misses Series 1-2

Dedication

For courageous girls and women who forge
their own paths, who aren't afraid to walk alone,
and make their unique mark upon this world.

Acknowledgements

Thanks to my inspiring assistants DF and CJ. Without you, I'd run in circles. As someone who has never owned a horse, I appreciate everyone who offered advice about horses and horse racing. My editors deserve much credit for helping me polish HOW TO WIN A DUKE'S HEART, and as always, the feedback from my review team continues to help me write books readers enjoy.

1

Ayr, Scotland

Belleisle Racecourse

7 August 1810—half past ten in the morning

Eager for any sight of the sleek racehorses, Sophronie Slater leaned forward on the luxurious gold velvet seat until her nose practically touched the glass. As she peered out the coach's dusty windows, butterflies giddily flitted around her tummy.

How she loved the races. Ever so much more than stuffy, pompous balls, routs, and soirees.

Only Scottish-bred horses were permitted to run the Belleisle track, and she was curious to learn how the horseflesh would measure up against the thoroughbreds she and her father raised in America. Or against the impressive high steppers Papa had purchased while they'd been in England these past months.

Remorse prodded her conscience when she considered the ocean voyage the poor beasts would have to endure, secured in the ship's bowels for weeks on the return journey to Virginia. Papa had cautioned her against purchasing too many horses for that very reason.

So far, Sophronie had only bought a lovely broodmare at Tattersall's a few weeks ago. On the other hand, Father had made several purchases, including a trio of sinewy racehorses: two colts and a filly.

However, she was too excited about today's race to remain downcast for more than a passing moment. Unlike some breeders or racehorse owners, the Slaters prided themselves on taking the very best care of their animals.

Sophronie scrutinized the scenery as the coach slowly trundled along. The coachmen called out harsh warnings to anyone or anything in the path of the brilliant matched black team. Other drivers cursed and shouted as they too maneuvered wagons, carriages, dog carts, and all manner of other conveyances through the growing throng.

A man hurried past with a boy on his shoulders of perhaps five or six years and clutching a bright red and blue top. Two grinning older lads trotted behind them, each waving a cup and ball toy. A woman who might've been their mother, carrying a toddler with glossy raven curls and her thumb stuck in her mouth, followed at a more sedate pace. From their tidy but plain attire, Sophronie guessed them to be local villagers on an outing.

Farther along, two couples dressed in the first stare of fashion strolled along, preening in the attention they received. The ladies twirled their lacy parasols as their menfolk strutted behind them like proud peacocks.

Racecourses brought all manner of people together. For a few hours, social class and position were forgotten and spectators, rich and poor alike, cheered for their favorite horse.

Would the surly Duke of Waycross be there today?

Did hungry piglets squeal?

Sophronie released a forceful, indelicate snort, and Papa issued a warning. "Ahem."

"Pardon me, Papa."

Sending him a contrite smile, she adjusted her position on the seat to better see out the small window. A fly landed on the glass, crawling a convoluted path until a wheel sank into a rut, jarred the conveyance, and sent the insect on its way. Fine dust particles crept into the well-made coach, and the promise of a warm day and the large crowd might've put a less robust woman off.

Sophronie searched the cottony cloud-ridden azure sky.

It was a perfect day for a horse race.

She lived for events like these. No, she thrived on activities of this nature; outdoors, away from the rigid strictures of Society, and in the proximity of horses.

What could be better?

What more could she desire?

Only one thing.

The day would be far more enjoyable if she didn't have to worry about encountering the disagreeable Duke of Waycross.

Of course the craggy-faced, imposing Scot would be here, stomping around and scowling at everyone and everything. Waycross also raised and raced horses, and usually that would've exalted him to a lofty status in her estimation. Nevertheless, a more unpleasant man Sophronie had never met. His love of horseflesh couldn't compensate for his gruff temperament and severe presence.

In truth, she'd never seen the duke smile.

Scowl, frown, smirk, sneer, deride, mock, curse, and grimace?

Oh, aye. Many, *many* times. But a genuine smile of warmth or humor? Not once. Not even a nascent upward tip of his firm lips.

What caused a man to be that grim and humorless?

"We're only here to observe the race today, my girl," Papa said by way of warning for at least the third time. They were to return home at the end of August, and securing accommodations for any more horseflesh aboard a ship bound for Virginia might prove difficult.

"I know, Papa," Sophronie responded, her attention still fixed on the teeming grounds.

A stunning raven-haired woman atop a sidesaddle, and wearing an elegant empire-style raspberry-red riding habit adorned with black and silver accents, expertly guided her dun-colored mare toward the racetrack. The black scarf secured around the lady's jaunty top hat flowed behind her in the breeze like a banner as she rode.

A delicate black lace veil concealed her features, but there could be no doubting she was quality. Likely an aristocrat, given the alert and identically navy-blue and saffron-yellow-liveried footmen riding in her wake like soldiers guarding their queen.

Sophronie glanced down at her bottle-green and peony-pink striped traveling costume. A slight frown tugged her eyebrows together. The bright pink silk of her spencer was more appropriate for a walk in Hyde Park than a racecourse. Perhaps she ought to have worn a gown in a more subdued hue.

Giving a mental shrug, she turned her attention outdoors once more. It was too late to worry about her ensemble now. At least her fawn-colored half boots would serve her well. If she'd had her way, she'd have worn her boys' attire—including sensible boots that came to her knees. Skirts were so cumbersome. Men had no idea the freedom something as trivial as trousers provided them.

A race never failed to stir her blood, and today was no exception. Fortunately, the sport was widely admired by both males and females, and for a change, Sophronie's presence wouldn't be remarked upon. No male would level her an affronted glare, mutter grievances beneath his breath, or declare a woman's attendance wasn't *de rigueur*.

Sophronie doubted she was capable of being *de rigueur*, and if that truth offended *le beau monde's* stodgy sensibilities, she didn't give two farthings. She wasn't English, and the approval of the upper ten thousand meant nothing to her. However, her father was of a different opinion.

She cast him a swift glance only to find him studying her again as he relaxed against the posh squabs. He'd done that often of late, particularly since they'd come to England. Fiddling with the silk cord of her pink crocheted and beaded reticule, she speculated for the umpteenth time whether he'd anticipated she'd find a husband on this trip. After all, she was nearly three and twenty.

Surely Papa understood she couldn't marry an Englishman and live far away from her beloved father. She'd never entertained the notion finding a husband in England, not even for half a second. Her home was in Virginia and her husband, should there ever be one, would be an American.

She'd met plenty of pleasant, friendly people in England. Indeed, she'd made a few dear friends she would write to for the rest of her life. But the truth of it was, Sophronie was too different, too untamed, too unrefined to truly fit into English society. What was more, she didn't want to. The strictures, rules, and expectations were suffocating at best and hypocritical at worst.

As George Slater's only surviving child, Papa had cosseted her. They both knew he had. There'd been a boy and girl born to Sophronie's parents before her birth. Elias and Molly had died from a fever, as had Mama a week later when Sophronie had been a toddler.

If it weren't for the family portrait, painted shortly before her mother, sister, and brother had fallen ill, she'd not know what they looked like. Her memories of them had faded with time until barely any details remained. Regret filled her as they'd become hazy images she couldn't see clearly. It grieved and frightened her that she could forget people she'd loved so very much.

It was unfair—no, cruel.

Time had robbed her of those precious memories. Some people claimed the passing of time was a blessing—*time heals all wounds*—but time also stole irreplaceable recollections. In truth, Sophronie believed she would rather feel the pain if it meant her memories remained intact.

Well aware of how often Papa indulged her whims, she tried not to take advantage of his affection. After the death of her siblings and Mama, Sophronie and Papa had grown ever closer.

As he had no sons, George Slater permitted her to learn the intricate business of raising and breeding horseflesh. An uncommon practice which offended the genteel sensibilities of their neighbors, his pompous cronies, and nearly everyone in New England in any way associated with horse breeding or racing, but which made her adore him all the more.

She'd excelled at both equine breeding and racing and had become an accomplished jockey to boot. That was a source of pride for Sophronie and her father but a pebble in the shoe of many other men. Particularly a rugged Scotsman's large, scuffed boots. Men didn't take kindly to a woman besting them at anything, and most especially not a sport generally reserved for males.

George Octavius Slater was a fair man—an honest man. A man of faith, integrity, and honor. He didn't boast about his self-made wealth, nor did he look down upon those who were less fortunate.

In point of fact, he was somewhat of a champion for the underdog, and he expected his hoyden of a daughter to act with kindheartedness and graciousness at all times. Papa might excuse Sophronie's lack of decorum, but ill humor or meanness was unacceptable.

Papa had long ago given up shaping her into a respectable young woman of high station, although Sophronie could pass for a polished lady when circumstances required it. He might disapprove of her riding astride in breeches, participating in horse races, bidding at Tattersall's, and any number of other unladylike pursuits, but still he loved her and tolerated her wild nature.

Only so far as it came to her love of horses, however.

A wicked grin twitched the corners of Sophronie's mouth, and she angled her head so that her bonnet's brim hid her smirk from her father.

She'd outbid that brusque Scotsman, Evan Gordonstone, Duke of Waycross, at Tattersall's, and he had yet to forgive her. Even after he'd secured that magnificent Friesian from the Gypsy travelers in June, despite Sophronie's best efforts to buy the stallion.

In truth, she hadn't intended to use the horse for breeding stock but rather her own mount. Nevertheless, common sense had eventually prevailed because not only was the stallion too large for her small frame, she couldn't bear the notion of him being confined below a ship's deck for weeks.

An animal as powerful and regal as the Friesian ought to be running free in verdant pastures, his glossy ebony mane and tail waving in the wind. Her smug smile faded, replaced by an almost peeved frown. *Almost*, except she wouldn't give Waycross the satisfaction, even if the boor wasn't present to see her peevishness.

The triumphant glint in his blue-gray eyes when she'd finally conceded the horse to him had almost been enough to change her mind about allowing the duke the stallion. She possessed the funds to outbid Waycross. The ornery man certainly didn't deserve any leniency or sympathy from her after the impolite, disdainful manner in which he'd treated her these many weeks.

Regardless, Sophronie had recognized the immediate bond between Waycross and the stallion. A melding together of majestic animal and a man more feral beast than sophisticated duke. That type of unity was rare and heartwarming.

Truth be told, she hadn't believed Waycross capable of the gentler emotions she'd witnessed playing across his angular face that June afternoon when he haggled with the Gypsy over the stallion's price.

The duke had never been anything but icily civil to

her—just barely at that. No, he'd been downright hostile at the Gypsy encampment when he'd bought the Friesian.

Regardless, she would not permit him to ruin this glorious day.

Little dust clouds kicked up here and there as all manner of vehicles lumbered about, searching for a place to deposit their occupants or to park. Hawkers called their wares from crude, temporary booths set up along the perimeter of the makeshift lane.

She perked up and squinted at a stand.

Was that toffee?

Sophronie made a mental note to purchase the delicious confection before she left. She readily admitted she had a sweet tooth, but only for specific treats. Topping the list were toffee, pralines, and sweet potato pie. Just thinking about the desserts made her mouth water, despite her hearty breakfast.

Perhaps she'd purchase the toffee straightaway, lest the merchant sell out quickly.

A quartet of lads ran by, laughing and hollering. A brown dog of indeterminable breeding yapped at their heels.

The air fairly tingled with excitement and expectation.

After a rather tipsy gentleman doffed his hat at her, Sophronie drew back into the shadow of the coach's interior. Even she wasn't unwise enough to encourage a tippler's foxed attention.

Unsurprisingly, none of the racehorses were visible amid the congestion of conveyances and crowd of spectators. She slid a glance to her father, tranquil with ankles crossed and hands folded upon his stomach.

His gray-peppered mustache quivered as he attempted to appear solemn.

"We're not here to buy horses, Roni," Papa reminded her again, using his pet name for her.

Grinning, she cocked her head as she pulled her gloves up. "Unless, of course, *you* see an animal *you* cannot resist."

"No. Not this time, my dear." Shaking his head, he chuckled. "I came at Waycross's behest."

That brought Sophronie up short. She paused in adjusting her embroidered green satin gloves. "The Duke of Waycross?"

Why hadn't he said as much before?

Probably because he knew she'd object.

Papa merely lifted a satirical eyebrow. "I'm not acquainted with any other gentleman of that name. Are you?"

He well knew she wasn't.

She tried not to sound as flummoxed as she felt. "He sought *your* opinion?"

And not hers?

Well, why should he have done? After all. She was a woman, and "women have nae place raisin' horseflesh or imposin' themselves upon male pursuits."

She'd heard Waycross angrily mutter those very words and hadn't a doubt he'd meant for her to overhear him.

The coach groaned to a rocking halt.

"Yes, he did." Papa straightened and adjusted his hat. He looked rather dapper. He was still a handsome man, but he'd shown no interest in remarrying after Mama's death. "He has his eye on two horses and wanted my opinion as to which would be the better stud."

"Oh."

Disappointment engulfed the coach, muting Sophronie's earlier exuberance.

That meant she would indeed see Waycross today.

They *would* quarrel.

It was inevitable as water running downhill toward the sea.

Sophronie and Waycross always did. No matter how determined she was to not react to the duke's deliberate goading, as predictably as a match touched to tinder burst into flames, she lost her temper. What was more, she couldn't deny a surge of triumph when irritation sparked in his stormy eyes. There was something most satisfying about getting beneath the severe duke's sun-browned skin.

The coach bounced and squeaked as one of the stocky drivers descended to open the conveyance's door.

"Pet, I know you and the duke have been at cross purposes. But I believe Waycross is a decent man. An upstanding and honorable man." Papa winked. "You won't like hearing it, Roni, but the pair of you are very much alike in many ways."

The door swung open.

"Are you daft, Papa?" Sophronie couldn't help her disrespect or raised pitch. Shock and surprise had a way of sending one's voice to the ceiling and making one forget one's manners. "I am *nothing* like the Duke of Waycross. He's a growly, cantankerous bear. His teeth and claws are always bared and ready to draw blood. Usually mine."

"Sophronie." Papa's tone turned stern, a warning in his tenor. "That is beneath you."

It was true nonetheless.

"Never fear, Papa. I shall behave today. I give my word."

The irascible Duke of Waycross would find no fault with her comportment this day. For her father's sake, Sophronie fully intended to be the quintessence of serene decorum in the duke's presence. She would staunchly refuse to be drawn into a verbal sparring match. Even if it meant she had to bite her tongue. Literally.

She angled toward the exit and froze, a groan

lodging in her throat.

Fiddlesticks.

No, not fiddlesticks. That was far, far too tame an expletive.

Bloody, bloody hell.

Papa hadn't been warning her to behave today but rather cautioning her to hold her tongue *now*.

In all of his imposing ruggedness, Evan Gordonstone, Duke of Waycross, had opened the coach door. But of course he had. The man had the most exasperating habit of appearing wherever Sophronie least wanted him to be.

She summoned a smile so disingenuous, her facial muscles twitched in betrayal.

Perchance he hadn't heard her unflattering outburst.

His features granite hard and just as inflexible, Waycross raised an imperial, slashing black eyebrow.

"Sorry to disappoint ye, but there havena been bears in Scotland since the fifth century or thereabouts, Miss Slater."

2

Still Belleisle Racecourse
A few awkward moments later

Blocking the coach opening, Evan leaned a shoulder against the frame. His posture was rude and intimidating. Regardless, the American lass deserved everything he dealt her and more. Sophronie Slater had been a source of vexation from the moment they'd met.

For a fleeting instant, chagrin swept across the smattering of freckles on her face before she swiftly adopted a nonchalant mien and fashioned a stiff smile. Her hydrangea-blue eyes, framed by dark ginger lashes, remained wide and unflinching—*challenging*—as always.

He didn't think her capable of coyness or diffidence. Miss Slater's directness marked her as an American even before she opened her mouth and her cultured southern drawl emerged.

"In point of fact, perceived aggression by *bears* is usually the creature actin' defensively when it feels threatened," Evan said. A not-so-subtle strike, but she made it so deliciously easy.

Her eyes flashed with blue fire at the unspoken insinuation, but for once, Miss Slater kept her opinion to herself. A miracle that. All of the angels and saints in heaven must be rejoicing.

"Waycross." George Slater nodded, his judicious gaze swinging between his daughter and Evan. The man was no idiot. He recognized the tension.

"Slater." Evan dipped his chin. He respected Slater and had no wish to make an enemy of the man over his impulsive and fractious offspring.

It would've been too much to expect George Slater to leave his impudent daughter with one of her English friends while the American visited Scotland. Evan hadn't thought to request that very thing. Truthfully, he doubted Slater would've considered joining him in Ayr had his daughter been excluded from the invitation.

More fool Evan for not having considered that fact and making arrangements to distract Miss Slater. His sisters would've done the trick nicely, and with a promise of a new bonnet apiece, they'd have kept this blue-eyed termagant well away from him all day. Too blasted bad he hadn't thought of that brilliant notion before.

His focus drifted to Slater.

The American's devotion to his daughter was evident to anyone with eyes in their head. As much as Miss Slater irritated Evan, he admired her father's affection for her. Evan's extended family was close-knit and loving too.

Nevertheless, Miss Sophronie Slater behaved like no other woman of Evan's acquaintance. Blessed with three sisters, four aunts, and two grandmothers—all living at Balston House—Evan *knew* women. Strong-minded and spirited, every one of his female kin paled in comparison to Miss Slater's sheer mulishness, impertinence, and complete disregard for what others thought of her.

Miss Slater was perplexing, aggravating, maddening, infuriating, and a dozen more unflattering terms.

"We have bears in Virginia, but it's rare to see one," she practically chirped. A bid, Evan would vow, to cover her ill-timed statement regarding his bearish nature.

Giving her a stern paternal warning with his gaze, George Slater descended from the coach. "Good of you to watch for us, Waycross. Saved us bustling about in this horde trying to find you."

At first glance a person might dismiss Slater, of average height and build, as…well, average. However, acute intelligence shone in his blue eyes, so very much like his impetuous daughter's. Rarely had Waycross come across a man with a keener mind, more brilliant business sense, or such an extraordinary eye for prime horseflesh.

In truth, George Slater's only shortcoming seemed to be the lackadaisical parenting that permitted his daughter's spitfire behavior.

Slater's knowledge of horses was precisely why Evan had requested his presence at the Belleisle Racecourse today. He coveted the man's insight on the stallions Evan was interested in. Neither was favored to win the race and in fact, both would retire from racing soon. Which was why he was considering one or the other as a stud.

Evan glanced behind him. The coachmen hovered a few feet away, apparently assuming Evan would assist Miss Slater from the conveyance.

Bollocks.

If Evan had his way, he'd lock the lass inside the coach until it was time for her father to depart. Pressing his mouth into a displeased line, he extended his hand. "Miss Slater."

Politesse was highly overrated. A deuced farcical expectation. Had Miss Slater's father not been present, Evan would've presented his back and stalked away.

For several blinks, Miss Slater simply stared at his black-gloved palm.

Evan quirked an eyebrow in challenge.

She wanted to refuse his help as much as he disliked

offering it.

He saw the reluctance in her pretty eyes and the way she pursed her plump lips. But Evan had heard her promise to behave with his own ears. Snubbing him mere minutes after her arrival meant she'd either lied or wasn't capable of controlling herself.

Personally, Evan would bet his scuffed boots on the latter.

She gave a resigned sigh, placed her small hand in his, and permitted him to help her alight.

Her temperament was so overbearing, he quite forgot how delicate of form she was. The top of her head barely reached his shoulder. What she lacked in height, she made up for in sheer doggedness and temerity. Oddly, he admired those qualities in his female relatives, but in Miss Slater, they rubbed raw as thistle prickles on his bare arse.

The instant her booted feet touched the ground, she removed her hand from his with such alacrity, he might've had leprosy or offensive body odor.

Annoyed despite himself, Evan clasped his hands behind his back.

Many women would've used their wiles to find an excuse to extend the moment. Evan knew his worth. Aye, he was Scots, and his coffers were nearly empty, but he was an eligible duke nonetheless.

Women had been angling to become his wife from the moment he'd inherited the title. Leah Wesleyan had no qualms about her blatant interest in becoming the next Duchess of Waycross. She eyed him with the concentration and prowess of a feral cat stalking a nestling, waiting for the opportunity to pounce.

Evan had little interest in silly women with no thought in their heads besides the latest frippery they'd purchased or the juiciest gossip they'd heard of late. He'd resisted marrying an heiress to fill the duchy's empty coffers. He'd much prefer to restore the estate to prosperity by his own merit.

Miss Slater tucked her parasol under one arm and adjusted her reticule as she examined her surroundings. She fairly vibrated with excitement, and he almost smiled at her contagious enthusiasm. She reminded him of himself…once upon a time.

"The pair of you are very much alike in many ways."

Slater's words from a few minutes earlier played through Evan's mind. Perhaps there was more truth in that statement than either he or Miss Sophronie Slater realized.

Or wanted to admit.

At least Evan could credit her with a rational brain. She was almost as obsessed with equines as he—her only redeeming quality. From half-closed eyelids, he observed her.

Azure eyes alight with interest, she gazed about, her attention landing here and there before darting to something else. Evan recognized the instant she spotted a few of the gleaming racehorses being led by their jockeys toward the track.

Her pink mouth parted on a soft, delighted, "Oh."

He well understood her fascination. As a young lad, he'd been entranced with horseflesh. As an adult, struggling for the past five years to make a successful go of breeding and racing to support his extended family and extensive estate, he'd become less sentimental and more unrepentantly logical.

"The first heat doesna begin for almost an hour. Would ye care to visit the stables for a few minutes?"

Evan asked. "We shall have to take care no' to intrude upon the jockeys and owners, but I can direct ye to the two horses I am considerin' purchasin'."

"Indeed," Slater said with a smile and twinkle in his eye. "There's nothing like a race day, is there?"

Evan glanced around as if seeing his surroundings for the first time.

He used to enjoy this—looked forward to a race as eagerly as a Scottish lad or lass unwrapping their Hogmanay gifts or an English child their Christmastide presents. Now, however, so much depended on whether he made the best selection of studs and broodmares… Och, the joy had been stolen from what he'd once been most passionate about.

When one had several mouths to feed and had become the sole means of support for numerous people, that rather put a damper on frivolous betting and casual breeding he'd dabbled in when he'd been the spare and not the heir. His deceased father and elder brother had nearly bankrupted the dukedom, leaving him to pick up the shattered remnants and glue the jagged pieces back together.

Evan would be damned if he'd be as irresponsible,

negligent, or reckless as those two had been. He had duties. Responsibilities. Obligations. His own needs and wants were secondary to preserving the duchy.

What was more, he had limited funds to build the stock he prayed would enable him to make a name for himself in breeding and racing circles. The horses and stables were his means of reversing the failing estate he'd inherited. By damn, he'd not give up until he'd exhausted every resource or avenue to achieve his goal.

Hence, he'd swallowed his pride and asked George Slater for his opinion on the studs. The man might be an American, but he knew horses. The man was likely the most knowledgeable about horseflesh of all Evan's acquaintances.

Honestly, he welcomed Slater's expertise.

His daughter's all too easily given viewpoints Evan could well do without.

If Evan failed to make a go of his breeding ventures within the next couple of years, he'd have to seriously consider marrying an heiress.

Leah Wesleyan's wide eyes and porcelain features intruded.

Aye, Leah was beautiful and an heiress. She knew exactly how a lady of quality ought to conduct herself. She was also coldly calculating and self-centered.

Slater extended his arm toward Miss Slater. "Shall we, my dear?"

"Oh, yes." She gave him a sunny smile, revealing her slightly crooked front teeth. Their minor imperfection didn't detract from her pixyish prettiness. Her eyes flashing with eagerness, she looped her hand through her father's elbow.

A little chap holding a toy top waved at her.

Grinning, Miss Slater waved back.

She liked children.

Evan wasn't surprised. Hardly bigger than a child herself, Sophronie Slater embraced life with the same enthusiasm and innocence that children did.

A loud bang reverberated, causing a few nearby women to scream and men to swear.

Scowling, Evan craned his neck to see where the sound had originated. Nothing unusual or suspicious met his perusal. Noises of that caliber could send an edgy horse into a panic.

Miss Slater also swiftly glanced around, the pink feathers tucked into the rim of her pink bonnet fluttering in the breeze. "The air is so bracing here, the landscape majestic, especially the hillsides strewn with heather, and the people warm and friendly."

She acted as if she hadn't even heard the explosion or whatever it had been. Or else she had heard it and remained remarkably composed.

Evan grudgingly permitted a jot of respect for her comportment. The truth of it was, he'd never seen Sophronie Slater respond with histrionics, dramatics, or other female machinations.

What a bloody, blessed relief.

Regardless, she had a tongue sharp enough to strip the bark from a Scotch pine and a wit devilish enough to cause Satan to roll his eyes in vexation.

Recalling her previous jab about his temperament, Evan snorted. "That's no' what most people say about us Scots."

"*Really?*" One red-gold brow raised impishly, mockery riddling her tone. She put a gloved finger to her chin and looked coyly thoughtful. "I suppose it's a case of the proverbial rotten apple giving everyone a bad name."

No need to ask whom she directed that barb toward, nor was there a need to point out she'd mixed her expressions. Although Evan might enjoy her reaction if he were boorish enough to do the latter.

Nae, he'd called a silent truce for the day.

If Miss Slater was on her best behavior today, then Evan would be as well.

"Father, do we have time to explore Scotland before we leave for home?"

"Perhaps a couple of days at most this trip, my dear," Slater agreed with an affectionate glance. "But no more. We have the return journey to England and preparations to return to Virginia to complete."

Something unnamable and highly peculiar battered Evan's ribs.

"Ye're returnin' to America?"

Naturally, they must. The Slaters had been away several months. Evan scratched behind his ear. The truth he wanted to deny knifed into his gut like a rusty sword. He would miss the bickering and bantering with Miss Slater.

How could that be? She irritated him like no other.

No one enjoyed verbal sparring. Was he off his bloody, sodding head?

~*~

What a perverse conundrum.

"Aye, we are. At the end of the month," Slater confirmed as he fell into stride beside Evan. "We're taking several beautiful horses back with us."

Including Beville's broodmare that Evan had his eye on for two years. Miss Slater had bought the mare out from under him, but she'd not succeeded in getting her pretty hands on Eclipse. The Friesian had become Evan's favorite mount. In fact, the horse was here today, tucked away in the stables.

As they made their way toward the enclosure, he surveyed the crowd. The usual rabble-rousers were present. The privileged dandies, coxcombs, and fops who drank too much, bet funds they often didn't possess, heckled the jockeys, frightened the horses, and made lewd overtures to any female under the age of sixty.

As they approached the stables, Evan's head stable hand, Brody McFarland, came forward.

"Yer Grace. Eclipse is in high fettle." He sent a blistering glower and jabbed his thumb toward a cluster of finely dressed young bloods.

As Evan watched, two fribbles took long swigs from silver flasks, then passed them to their soused cohorts. Drunk as wheelbarrows before noon.

"One of those English scunners lit a firework at the stable's north end. Kilburn and McArdle are tryin' to soothe the laddie. Other beasties are worked up too. It'll likely affect the racin' today. I'd be bound that miserable lot are countin' on it."

"Goddammit!" Evan didn't give ten damns that he'd sworn in front of a lady. His care was for the horseflesh. In any event, he'd wager Miss Slater had heard far worse, considering the company she kept.

"That's terrible. Simply unacceptable. There's no excuse for such cruelty." She narrowed her flashing blue eyes, and before Evan or her father knew what she was about, she stomped toward the rowdy young bucks. "You there."

Four of the wastrels turned toward her. Slow, lascivious grins split their inebriated countenances.

The devil fly away with them.

"Yes, you feckless, reckless ruffians." She gripped her parasol like a small, frilly saber and pointed it at them. "You should be ashamed of yourselves."

"Well, chaps, what do we have here?" the tallest fellow murmured, hands planted on his hips.

Evan fisted his hands into tight balls. God, how he wanted to punch him in the face and knock him into next summer. That would wipe away that lewd smile and the licentious glint from the cad's eyes.

"A pretty little American, Radford, if I don't miss my mark," another libertine said, boldly ogling Miss Slater.

"You *never* miss your mark, Hastings." The tall chap sniggered.

The four men passing the flasks around erupted in gales of laughter and slapped each other on the shoulders. Three other rapscallions crouched in a circle, attempting to light a firecracker.

Jesus Christ on the bloody cross.

Those rotters ought to be beaten black and blue for terrifying horses in such a vicious manner, not to mention discharging an explosive with so many people about. Sheer lunacy. Someone could've been maimed or killed.

He curled his lip in scorn.

Stupid, stupid sods.

"Sophronie. Come back here." George Slater took off after his impetuous daughter.

No doubt he knew as well as Evan did that once the chit got a notion in her head, nothing short of the Almighty himself appearing and telling her to desist would dissuade her. In all likelihood, she'd argue with God himself if she believed herself right.

"Shite." Forget what Evan had thought earlier about Sophronie Slater having a rational brain. He swung to face McFarland. "Find security and tell them *I* want that riffraff removed at once." He stabbed a finger toward the chortling gentlemen. "They are banned from Belleisle."

After all, Evan was a duke. A duke's word went a very long way. No doubt there was a lord or two or three amongst those pasty-faced swains, and they'd balk at being expelled. Their papas would pad the right pockets, and the profligates would be back, causing trouble at the next event.

Nevertheless, they'd be banished for the rest of today, and that was sufficient for now.

"Have either San Sebastian or Heatherston arrived?" Both were also Scottish dukes and fast friends of Evan's. Whenever their duties permitted them the time, they arranged to meet.

"Nae, Yer Grace." McFarland spat on the ground to indicate his disgust with the snickering popinjays. "Someone needs to teach them bloody blighters manners."

Or pound some common sense into the sots.

Mouth pursed, Evan swiftly strode after the dervish in striking green and pink. He tried his damnedest not to notice the enticing sway of her nicely rounded hips as she marched toward her quarry. A vibrant, enraged wee bird about to take on a pack of wolves.

"Sophronie!" her father called again when the firecracker's fuse lit then sputtered out. Holding his hat, and his face creased in consternation, he quickened his pace. Slater had also seen the trio's nefarious plot and realized the peril to his infuriated but oblivious daughter.

A pair of jockeys exited the stables, each leading a quivering horse well away from the troublemakers. One of the jockeys also spat at the scalawags and swore in French. "*Imbéciles stupides.*"

A young blood let out a triumphant whoop, and guffawing and hooting, the rest dashed several feet away.

Sophronie stumbled to a stop, her gaze riveted on the firework's sizzling fuse.

Bloody hell.

"Miss Slater!" Evan broke into a sprint. "Sophronie, get away. Now!"

She swiveled toward him, her tormented blue eyes huge and, for once, filled with indecision.

"*Roni*, run. Run, Roni!" her father called, racing toward her, fear rendering him hoarse.

Longer-legged, Evan passed him in a trice. With a gravelly, guttural shout, he seized Sophronie in his arms and bolted in the other direction.

The firework exploded a second later, sending debris and cinders over his back and head. Once more, women shrieked, men shouted curses, bairns wailed, and horses screamed in terror.

By God, Evan would have those miscreants charged with reckless endangerment and any other crime he could think of.

Sophronie cried out and strained against him.

Had she been burned?

Hot sparks seared Evan's head and ears. His hat had fallen off when he'd charged toward her.

The shouting and shrieking continued to permeate the air.

"Papa." Sophronie struggled like a madwoman in Evan's arms. "Papa! Put me down, you brute. Papa's hurt."

Slowly, Evan pivoted, his attention snagging on the prostrate man.

His breath stuck in his throat.

George Slater lay motionless, pale as chalk, with blood gushing from a head wound.

3

Outside Glasgow, Scotland
Balston House—six hours later

*P*lease, God. Please don't let Papa die.

Sophronie sat on the edge of her father's oversized bed. Picking up his limp hand, she fought back the hot tears smarting her eyes. Crying would change nothing and leave her gritty-eyed, woolly-headed, and more wretched than she already felt.

Her strong, healthy father lay motionless and as pale as the stark white bandages encircling his head. She pressed the back of her hand to her mouth to stifle the animalistic cry clawing its way up her throat.

Late afternoon sunlight filtered through the leaded-glass windows, bathing the well-appointed room in a myriad of miniature rainbows. Typically, such a beautiful sight would've delighted Sophronie. Just now, she couldn't summon the tiniest smile or even appreciate the Duke of Waycross's magnificent castle.

She glanced around, taking in the twelve-foot-high ceiling, the egg-and-dart crown molding, and the luxurious, if outdated, heavy mahogany furnishings.

This was no house, despite the structure's unpretentious name. Always fascinated with the past, she typically would've questioned Waycross about the keep's history and construction, his ancestors, whether the castle was haunted, if battles had been fought upon his lands, and so much more.

But she'd barely spared him a word since her arrival, so concerned was she for her father.

George Slater hadn't stirred at all.

Not when the Duke of Waycross's men had carried him to the coach. Not on the agonizingly slow journey to the duke's home. Not when Waycross's footmen removed his clothing in exchange for a nightshirt—likely the duke's—or even when the spry doctor examined him and tended Papa's wounds.

Upon seeing Papa insensate on the ground, the duke had taken immediate command of the situation. He'd sent one of his men to fetch the physician, another to Balston House with orders for them to make rooms ready for Sophronie and her father, and…

She pressed two fingers to the bridge of her nose.

What else?

Sophronie's mind was a complete muddle—a hazy fog shrouded her brain. She pressed her palm to her forehead and squeezed her eyes shut. She couldn't clearly remember the rest of what had happened.

However, for the first time, she was eternally grateful for the duke's imperiousness. He'd even thought to send a footman to the hotel where she and Papa had stayed last night in Glasgow to fetch their belongings. With his kindness and consideration, he'd ruined her illusion of him as an unbearable brute.

At least temporarily. No doubt Waycross would say or do something shortly to reinstate her opinion of him as a cantankerous dunderhead.

After Waycross had eased her down and they'd both rushed to her father's side, her mind had gone oddly numb. There'd been so much blood. Papa's blood. How could a person survive after losing that much blood? Even now, the memory made her want to retch, and she broke into a cold sweat as a wave of nausea tumbled her stomach over.

The next thing Sophronie knew, she'd been inside her father's coach, pressing a neckcloth to his wound— the duke's neckcloth. She didn't recall Waycross untying the starched strip and stuffing it into her shaking hands.

Scrunching her nose, she sorted through what she did remember.

Someone said the firework explosion had startled nearby horses, and they'd bolted. One animal, wild with fear, had plowed into Papa and then accidentally stepped on him in the ensuing mayhem. In addition to the laceration on the left side of his head, Papa suffered cracked ribs, a bruised sternum and spleen, and a broken hand.

The kindhearted physician, Norton Dargavel, had taken her aside and gently explained, "I dinna ken if yer father has other internal injuries, Miss Slater. I canna detect any, but in cases such as this, one can never be certain. Hopefully, he awakens soon, and I can question him." He skimmed his professional gaze over her father. "Undetected internal bleeding concerns me the most."

He didn't need to say such a scenario could be fatal. It was there, in his compassionate gaze and the gentling of his brogue.

Running her loving gaze over her father from his bandaged head to his feet tucked beneath a forest green and gold counterpane, Sophronie had puzzled her forehead.

"What should I do if he awakens, Doctor?"

She'd assumed the white-haired physician—with eyes so icy blue it was like looking into the brightest summer sky—would return to Glasgow.

He'd patted her shoulder in a grandfatherly fashion.

"Dinna fash yerself, lass. I'll stay the night and look in on him every couple of hours." He winked and closed his leather bag. "Nae one makes better Scotch pies than Mrs. Barnes. Pastry so flaky, ye'd swear ye'd gone to heaven." He patted his paunchy belly. "And her marmalade would make a saint cry. It truly would."

Sophronie angled her head to see the small brass clock atop the other nightstand. Had two hours passed since Doctor Dargavel had left her?

He'd be back soon then.

"Wake up, Papa. Please wake up."

Her voice broke, and she swallowed hard against her grief and fear.

She couldn't fathom life without her father—what it would be like to be totally alone in the world. *No. No. I shan't countenance it.* She refused to consider he might not awaken and fully recover. She had no one else. He must get well.

"How is he, lass?"

Startled, for she hadn't heard the duke's approach, Sophronie gasped and turned her head in his direction.

Waycross stood silhouetted in the doorframe. His large form nearly filled the entry. Running a hand through his black hair, he wandered farther into the chamber. Generally, his presence agitated her, but at this moment, he brought with him an unexpected sense of comfort.

"Unchanged, I fear," she said, wishing with all of

her being she could say otherwise.

"I'm sorrier than I can say."

Such genuineness underscored his words that Sophronie didn't doubt his sincerity. Papa and Waycross had always got on. *She* was the one the duke couldn't tolerate. After laying her father's hand down and smoothing the sheet across his chest, she lifted a shoulder.

"It's in no way your fault, Your Grace. In truth, I am solely to blame."

She swallowed against the fresh tightness closing her throat. Pain scissored her heart as guilt burrowed around in her chest. She *was* to blame.

If she hadn't gone off half-cocked, if she'd considered her actions before responding, if she'd listened to his calls to stop, Papa wouldn't be lying here. He wouldn't have been in the path of the frightened horse, and he wouldn't have been trampled by the frenzied animal.

Waycross didn't dispute her self-castigation, and that made Sophronie feel all the more guilty. Unfortunately, hind-sighted remorse was wholly unhelpful.

"Thank you for rescuing me, Your Grace. I shudder to think what would've happened if you hadn't."

He'd been all hard, sinewy muscles and masculine power when, in one svelte movement, he'd scooped her into his iron-like arms as if she weighed no more than a newborn lamb and pelted away from the firework.

She studied his face, taken aback at the angry red welts on his left jaw, cheek, and ear.

"You were burned," she whispered, dismayed that another person had also been hurt because of her headstrongness.

He lifted his broad shoulders, causing the fabric encompassing them to pull taut. "Och, 'tis nothin'. I've experienced worse from a Guy Fawkes bonfire."

"I'm truly sorry." Remorse and chagrin kicked a vicious, unrelenting staccato against the wall of her chest.

Hands behind his back, the duke stood on the opposite side of the bed, commanding but not intimidating. He'd changed into a casual fawn-colored jacket like those the villagers wore.

"My mother, grandmothers, and sisters are all prayin' for his recovery. Ye'll find they are a prayin' lot. There's a chapel in one of the other wings. If ye wish to visit, ye have only to ask, and someone will show ye the way." A tinge of a smile bracketed his mouth. "Grandmother Gordonstone also regularly calls the Almighty's wrath and Odin's curses down upon those who vex her."

Did he jest?

Sophronie would like to meet this feisty woman.

As if he'd read her mind, Waycross cut a wry glance to the open door. "She boasts Norse ancestors — Viking to be precise."

Sophronie hadn't been introduced to Waycross's family yet. They must think her an uncouth, ungrateful, ill-mannered colonial for following the men carrying her father straight up the stairs without so much as a hello.

"Please express my gratitude for all they have done and my apologies for not having introduced myself."

She met the duke's eyes.

For once, they weren't blue-gray tumult, shooting

angry daggers at her. If she didn't know better, she might've believed compassion and empathy shimmered in their depths. It must be the afternoon lighting playing tricks on her eyesight. His grace had never regarded her with anything but condescension and disparagement.

"I know I should thank them myself," she said, placing her hand upon her father's. "But I cannot bear to leave my father. I'm afraid that if I do…"

Emotion clogged her throat and choked her words. Words she couldn't bear to speak lest saying them aloud somehow would make what she most feared a reality. Her lower lip quivered, and she clamped it between her teeth to stop the tremors.

Crying in front of him was unthinkable. The ultimate humiliation.

Sophronie still wore her bloodstained gown, although she'd tossed her soiled gloves and spencer into a corner. At some point, a diligent servant had removed the ruined items. Her bonnet and reticule lay on the chair near the door where she'd dropped them upon entry.

"Have ye eaten?" Waycross continued to linger.

"No." She shook her head. Loose tendrils of hair

swung near her right cheek. "I'm not hungry."

"Ye'll need yer strength to nurse yer father back to health, lass." Those severe black eyebrows lashed together. "I'll have a bowl of cock-a-leekie soup sent up."

In the months she'd been acquainted with the duke, Sophronie had never known Waycross to take no for an answer. His highhandedness should've raised her ire, but her reserves were depleted. She didn't have the strength to argue with him.

Instead, she said, "Cock-a-leekie soup?" The name sounded highly suspicious. "What's in it?"

Cockroaches? Eels? Some other manner of awfulness?

Was this a mean trick, just when she'd started to let her guard down around him?

Waycross grinned, and the sight so flummoxed her, Sophronie stared, mouth slack. The transformation from gruff, hard-planed features into devastating masculine good looks left her speechless. And breathless, if she were wholly forthright.

No wonder he didn't smile often. Every woman

within view would turn into a cow-eyed nincompoop.

"It's no' but chicken soup." He scratched his nose. "The best ye've ever eaten, I'll wager." Eyeing her stained gown, he asked, "Have ye been shown yer chamber yet?"

She shook her head. "No. I couldn't leave my father."

"Lass, I'll sit with him. Ye go change. Ye'll feel better for it."

"No, I cannot—" How could he possibly think she could leave her father?

The duke held up his palm, silencing her protests. "It's next door, on the right. I've had bathwater sent up. Go freshen yerself, change out of yer soiled garments, and don somethin' comfortable. Afterward, I'll have a meal brought up to ye here, and ye *will* eat. Ye need to keep yer strength up. I'll no' have ye becomin' ill too. I dinna need two invalids to care for."

His brogue had thickened into a tantalizing tenor, and she couldn't be certain if a teasing lilt colored his last words or if his complaint was sincere.

Nevertheless, his grace was right, and she couldn't

begrudge him his justified concern. Papa was not the duke's responsibility. He was hers. She'd do all within her means to stay well and care for her father. And pray he made a swift and complete recovery.

Sophronie glanced toward the door, uncertainty about being away from her father vying with the desire to be rid of her bloodstained gown.

Could she bathe and return within twenty minutes?

Mayhap less because she wouldn't wash her hair, just plait it?

Yes. Yes, she could.

Slowly, she rose and reluctantly released her father's hand.

She drew in a deep breath to steady the fluttering in her stomach and unease causing her heart to beat an irregular rhythm. Shadows filled the corners of the room, foretelling the sun's setting.

Waycross sauntered to the fireplace and opened an embossed tin. He withdrew flint, steel, and tinder. After igniting a spark to light the spill, he touched the narrow twisted paper to a candle in a nearby sconce. Blowing out the spill, he lifted the candle from its gilded resting place then circled the chamber, lighting candles with the ease of someone accustomed to doing the task.

Sophronie had never taken him to be a coddled dandy, and he likely performed many menial tasks most gentlemen of the *ton* she'd been introduced to wouldn't consider doing for themselves.

Never had she imagined she'd ever owe a debt of gratitude to the Duke of Waycross or that she'd be a guest in his home. A forced guest, but nevertheless, a guest. He'd proved much more charitable toward her than she deserved.

"You will send for me if he awakens or if there is any change?" She swept several strands of hair that had worked free of her chignon behind her ear.

"Aye." Waycross nodded. "Bathe and change. I'll let ye ken if yer father so much as snores."

A hollow rendering of a smile bent her mouth. "I shall be back within the quarter hour."

Just as she finished speaking, Doctor Dargavel bustled through the doorway. His astute gaze traveled to Waycross.

"Miss Slater is goin' to bathe and change,"

Waycross offered by way of an explanation.

"We have things well in hand, Miss Slater." The doctor placed his battered bag on the foot of the bed. "Tend to yerself. Ye're nae good to yer father if ye fall ill too."

"So the duke has informed me." With a final perusal of Papa, she swept from the room, anxious to return as hastily as feasible.

Would she and her father be returning to Virginia at the end of the month? Should she send word to someone in London? There were so many details to see to if they remained in Scotland longer than expected.

She gave herself a mental shake. All of those concerns could wait until Papa awakened.

Upon overhearing the doctor's muffled voice filtering through the open doorway, she paused mid-stride.

"I dinna like the fact that he hasna awakened yet, Yer Grace. It doesna bode well."

Looking over her shoulder, she met the duke's sympathetic gaze before he firmly shut the door.

4

Balston House Dining Room

Two mornings later

Evan took a b racing sip of strong coffee as his mother and grandmothers entered the dining room. His sisters had arrived a few minutes ago and, after filling their plates from the sideboard, chatted excitedly about an upcoming ball a neighbor was hosting. Once his aunts entered, the chaos would be complete.

He'd already denied his sisters' entreaties for new ballgowns. How many ballgowns did a woman require? They had pouted prettily but then launched into ideas of how they each might freshen one of their current gowns.

As they crossed the polished floor, the older women

called good morning to the room at large.

"Good morning," Evan replied, cutting into a thick slice of ham.

His sisters echoed his greeting. Rosalind, his elder by one year, gave a distracted little wave to their mother and grandmothers. Sarah, three years younger than Evan's nine-and-twenty years, and Larissa, four years younger than Sarah, smiled but kept eating.

He eyed the doorway expectantly.

The aunties would sail in momentarily.

Ten women prattling like magpies might send a less tolerant man straight to his study or the stables. There were times Evan wished he had another brother or two, a male cousin, or an uncle about. But all in all, he didn't mind being outnumbered.

Perhaps Miss Slater would join them too.

George Slater had regained consciousness shortly after she'd returned to his chamber and had eaten half a bowl of cock-a-leekie soup that first night. Relieved but still concerned, Miss Slater hadn't been willing to leave his side all of this time.

However, Slater had requested a bath this morning.

Last night, Doctor Dargavel had said Slater might bathe if he were careful, had assistance from at least two male servants, and promptly returned to bed.

The physician still hadn't ruled out internal injuries other than the suspected bruised spleen, although there didn't appear to be any fresh concerns. It was difficult to tell where the source of his pain originated with the numerous welts and purple-yellowish marks covering Slater's torso and his broken ribs.

His dutiful and remorse-ridden daughter would have to vacate her father's chamber. It was high time she formally met Evan's family in any event. She'd seen Mother a few times in the corridor, but other than that, Miss Slater had been as reclusive as a nun at a brothel.

Blige, the butler, skillfully prepared tea for the older women and placed it at their preferred seats as they selected their breakfast. Mother sat at the foot of the table, his grandmothers to her left and right. The aunts sat on the right side of the table and his sisters on his left. No sooner had his mother and grandmothers situated themselves than Evan's aunts sailed in, four colorful schooners in full mast.

Mother's younger twin sisters, Christina and Mareona Larimore, had never married. Christina's affianced had broken off their betrothal a mere month before their nuptials and married an heiress. Mareona's heart belonged to a soldier who'd never returned from war.

Father's sisters, Katryne Kirkpatrick and Eufamie McCollister, had dutifully entered arranged marriages. Both childless when their husbands died several years ago, they'd adamantly refused to wed again. The women's aversion to the married state said much about the fallacies of wedded bliss.

True, Evan's parents' union had been a calculated business arrangement. However, unlike her sisters, Anna Gordonstone, Duchess of Waycross, had fallen in love with Andrew Gordonstone and he with her. Theirs might not have been a marriage made in heaven, but the joining had been a far cry from the cold, humiliating, and lonely arrangements the aunts had endured.

When he inherited the dukedom, Evan had invited all of the women to live at Balston House. They'd been so grateful for the invitation—none had been left financially secure—that they'd eagerly accepted. Each contributed what they could to the running of the estate, and no one complained at the economies they made in order to live together.

It was no easy task to feed Evan's family and the servants they employed.

Several moments passed as the women exchanged greetings and settled at the long table. As always in the summer months, a cheery bouquet of flowers from the gardens Mother so adored graced the center.

Mother smiled indulgently at her daughters presently discussing—*arguing*—about whether a woman could jump the hedges, fences, and other obstacles at the Wesleyans'.

Every year, the Wesleyans hosted a summer fair of sorts on their estate. This year's was scheduled to take place in three days, and of course, Evan and his family would attend. It was expected of him as the highest-ranking local aristocrat.

Competitions included archery, shooting, and an equestrian hunting course. Women and men competed separately, which always aggravated his female relatives. Aunt Katryne was a better shot than Evan, and nobody within a hundred miles could beat Larissa with a bow and arrow.

The prizes for those events were paltry compared to the tidy purse the winners of the equestrian course took home. The men's prize was considerably more than the women's, and his sisters were positive a woman could win the course.

Though excellent riders all three, Mother had expressly forbidden her daughters to take their mounts over anything higher than a mud puddle. A very shallow, very narrow mud puddle at that.

John, Evan's elder brother, had died after forcing his mount to take a jump too far across a creek. The horse had balked at the last moment and tossed John heel over arse. He'd struck his head upon a nearby boulder when he'd landed, dying instantly.

A mere six months prior, Father had died from complications brought on by an infected cut on his leg. John's death so soon afterward had struck the family hard. Until then, Evan had possessed no idea the estate was in such dire financial straits either.

Rosalind shook her head. Her burnished copper curls, left loose and hanging down her back, bounced with her vehemence. "I believe a skilled woman could," she insisted, holding her fork up for emphasis. "Women are no' given enough credit. They can do anythin' a man can."

"They canna sire children," Grandmother Gordonstone put in jovially before biting the end off a sausage dangling from her fork. "Or pee standin'."

"Mother Gordonstone," Mother chided, color infusing her rounded cheeks.

Exchanging an amused glance, Aunt Mareona and Aunt Eufamie chuckled.

In her youth, Grandmother Gordonstone had been almost as reckless and wild as Sophronie Slater.

His grandmother would adore Miss Slater. Evan was as confident of that fact as he was that his name was Evan Thomas Keith Gordonstone. What mischief those two could get into together.

"Dinna be a goose, Rosalind. It isna possible," Larissa scolded, a less vibrant version of her older sister.

Whereas Larissa's hair was more sable than auburn,

Sarah's was a light brown with a few ginger highlights. However, all three sisters both possessed the same dark brown eyes inherited from their sable-haired mother.

"I have to agree with Larissa," Sarah said with an apologetic glance to Rosalind as she speared a piece of boiled, herbed potato. "Nae woman ridin' sidesaddle could manage those heights."

"I might've done so astride," Grandmother Gordonstone declared with a dry chuckle.

Gold rimmed floral teacup poised at her mouth, Grandmother Larimore quirked a gray brow archly. "Ye were always a hoyden, Lizabeth. Even as a young girl ye liked nothin' better than to flout convention and shock everyone."

"And ye were always jealous of me, Canne," Grandmother Gordonstone retorted, though the twinkle in her eyes belied her tart response. "I had six offers of marriage, and ye only had four."

"Oh, do hush, and let us enjoy our meal," Mother gently admonished, accustomed to her mother and mother-in-law's bantering.

"I have to agree with Grandmother and Rosalind,"

Aunt Eufamie declared, her expression thoughtful. She idly moved her fork back and forth across her plate as Blige refilled empty teacups. "I believe it can be done."

Arms folded, Aunt Christina leaned back in her chair. "I ken of only one way to find out."

Mother went stock still. Slowly, she laid her fork down. "Absolutely, positively no'. I shall no' have it. Do no' even ask."

She speared each of her daughters with a the-subject-is-closed glare.

"But Anna, be reasonable. If one of us won the competition this year,"—Aunt Eufamie scooted her gaze around the table to include the younger women— "the prize money would feed us all for a good while."

Evan's heart stopped for a moment, and a combination of dismay and anger stabbed the organ. They shouldn't have to worry about such things. "I've told ye before, Aunt Eufamie, such matters are my worry."

"Oh, tosh," Sarah said, flapping her hand at him. "We're no' numbskulls, Evan. We ken funds are tight and how hard ye work to make ends meet." She slathered marmalade on a triangle of toast. "That a man should be burdened with providin' for his female kin, and they take nae responsibility in their own welfare and wellbein', is ludicrous."

He firmed his mouth. "No' so tight that any of ye should consider such a hazardous venture."

"I still say one of us could pull it off," Rosalind muttered mutinously. "I'd wager on it."

"Nae. That's my final word," Mother said. "It's far too perilous. Why, I've never heard of a woman jumpin' anything higher than three feet—sidesaddle *or* astride."

She picked up her fork, indicating the subject was closed.

"I have done so. Several times, in fact."

Of course ye have.

Sophronie would pick that precise moment to make an entrance.

As one, every person in the dining room swung their attention to the double doors.

Miss Slater hovered at the entrance, looking rather delectable in a soft cornflower blue gown with a creamy lace shawl about her shoulders. She'd tied her hair at her nape with a wide ivory bow. Ribbons of sunshine and fire shimmered in what Evan had, wrongly, believed unremarkable red-gold hair.

Except for faint purple shadows beneath her blue eyes, she looked rested and, more importantly, relieved. The fine lines of stress between her eyebrows and bracketing her mouth had disappeared.

"That wee lass jumps horses?" Grandmother Larimore trumpeted in what was meant to be a whisper. She was hard of hearing and had no idea she was so loud. "I canna believe it."

Sophronie moved hesitantly into the room. It suddenly struck Evan that this was the first time he'd seen her uncertain around other people. Heretofore she'd always presented herself with confidence many a man would envy.

At once, Evan stood and circuited the table. "Come in, Miss Slater. Allow me to introduce ye to my family."

The delicate flare of her lips turned upward in appreciation caused the weirdest sensation behind his breastbone. Pray God he wasn't ailing.

Evan quickly introduced her to his large family.

"I've been askin' the Good Lord to restore yer father's health, child," Grandmother Gordonstone said, taking Miss Slater's measure.

"We all have," Sarah put in with a friendly smile.

"Thank you." Sophronie returned her smile. "Papa is doing ever so much better. Please accept my apologies for not becoming acquainted sooner."

"Pish posh, my dear," Aunt Katryne said. "We understand completely. Family is everythin'."

Her eyes grew soft as she took in those around the table.

"Do dish up and join us, Miss Slater," Mother instructed.

Evan would wager she was grateful for their guest's timely interruption. It put an end to the discussion about the contest next week.

"Tea or coffee, miss?" Blige asked.

"Coffee with cream—that is, milk, please."

"Ah, yes. Ye Americans like yer coffee," Aunt Christina said. "Do ye really prefer it with cream rather than milk?"

As she added ham, potatoes, and toast to her plate,

Sophronie nodded. "Many Americans do. Some prefer molasses rather than sugar as a sweetener too."

There was only one empty chair beside Larissa and to Evan's left. He pulled out the chair, and she sank onto the seat. No sooner had she placed her napkin in her lap than Grandmother Gordonstone banged the table with the handle of her knife. "Tell me, lass. Have ye truly jumped a horse?"

Miss Slater cast Evan a swift, guarded glance.

With the merest shifting of his gaze, he sent her a silent message to say nothing on the subject, which, of course, she chose to ignore.

"Yes. Though I've never ridden a thoroughbred in a competition, in America, I've ridden horses on regular tracks as well as hunter's and other jumping courses."

"But do ye win, lass?" Grandmother Larimore asked dubiously. "Prettily trottin' a docile pony along a well-groomed path or riding sidesaddle doesna count."

After an almost indecipherable hesitation, Miss Slater nodded and studiously avoided looking in Evan's direction. "In America, yes. Several times, in truth."

"I told ye so," Rosalind said triumphantly. She

grinned at Miss Slater. "Ye're a woman after my own heart, Miss Slater."

"Fascinatin'," Larissa said.

"Miss Slater and her father raise and race horses in America." Evan tried to steer the conversation in another direction. Mother gripped her fork so tightly, her knuckles shone white, and she appeared on the verge of apoplexy. "She and I have had our sights set on the same horse more than once while they've been visitin'."

Aunt Christina gave Sophronie a shrewd, considering look. "Sounds like a match made in heaven to me."

"Indeed," Aunt Katryne inserted with a teasing smile. "A most brilliant match."

Only a dimwit could've missed their insinuation.

Color skated up Miss Slater's smooth cheeks, and she focused on cutting her ham.

Evan gave his aunts a warning look.

"What's that?" Grandmother Larimore bellowed. "Did ye say Evan and Miss Slater have made a match? Why dinna anyone tell me there is to be a weddin'?"

5

Balston House Library
9 August 1810—nearly midnight

Sophronie ought to be exhausted after only sleeping fitfully in short increments and having stayed by her father's bedside for two nights in a row. She *was* tired, but instead of slipping swiftly into the arms of Morpheus, her mind kept playing the humiliating scene at breakfast.

Did ye say Evan and Miss Slater have made a match? Why dinna anyone tell me there is to be a weddin'?

Unable to unwind and fall asleep, she'd decided a venture to the library in search of a book was just the thing. Something fusty, boring, and sure to make her drowsy. Perhaps an encyclopedia of agriculture maps and charts or a historical guide to bricklaying, stone masonry, and plastering.

Either was sure to have her dozing off within half an hour at most.

A book on animal husbandry, on the other hand, would keep her up again for a third sleepless night. That wouldn't do at all. She needed her wits about her. Not only to speak with Papa about when they'd return to England to prepare for the trip home but also in case she had to cross words with his grace again.

It shouldn't smart that the duke had been horrorstruck at the preposterous notion they were betrothed, but as pride had no gauge for sensibility, his undisguised shock did sting. Sophronie ordinarily didn't give a sailor's curse what others thought of her. She chalked her current sour mood and disgruntlement up to being overly tired, fretting about her father's health, her head whirling with the issues their delay would cause, and being amid strangers.

The runner along the corridor muffled her bare feet as she sped along. She'd forgotten to pack her slippers and nightrobe but ironically not her breeches, riding boots, shirt, and jacket. For modesty's sake, she'd thrown her coat over her nightgown, but she honestly didn't expect to encounter anyone at this hour.

She shoved her loose hair over her shoulder. Rarely did she plait the waist-length strands before retiring. She didn't like the ripples the braids left in her hair.

The castle had settled into slumber for the night. A comfortable contentedness and hominess filled the atmosphere. The sensation was unexpected in a structure as large and rambling as the keep.

The duke's household kept country hours, and everyone appeared to be snuggled fast in their respective beds. No yellow light seeped from beneath the doors as, the candle holder held high, she maneuvered through the passages and stairway. She'd glimpsed the library on her hasty charge from the coach to Papa's guest chamber that first day, else she'd not have known where it was in the labyrinth that was the Duke of Waycross's home.

Rather than eerie or unnerving, she found the castle's nocturnal creaks and groans oddly comforting.

How many generations of Waycrosses had walked these passageways; grown up in these imposing rooms; laughed, cried, and celebrated on these impressive grounds?

What were their stories? Their loves? Their losses?

What was the story behind his grace's aunts and grandmothers living with his family?

Sophronie was convinced there were intriguing tales there.

Her family history was a bit muddled and laid no claim to the aristocracy. Mama had been orphaned as an infant, and a kindly, childless couple had taken her in. Sophronie knew nothing about her mother's family. Papa's grandparents had immigrated from Germany to Virginia in 1717. They and his parents had died from yellow fever before Sophronie was born.

She'd like to have asked about the hunting course mentioned as she entered the dining room. Sophronie had competed in several races of that nature, but usually on her favorite horse, Cinnamon, in Virginia. If they were staying longer, she might be tempted to enter the contest and give the winnings to the duke's family.

From what she'd overheard, the duchy's finances weren't entirely stable. She better understood Waycross not outbidding her for the mare at Tattersall's now, and shame trotted her pointy heels across Sophronie's shoulders. Once again, she'd misjudged the man whose burdens appeared to be weighty.

Upon reaching the library, she cast a slightly guilty look behind her. Thanks to a dose of laudanum, Papa had been sleeping soundly when she'd checked on him at ten. She might be overstepping her hosts' hospitality by helping herself to a book, but no one had told her she couldn't, either.

If she were caught, she would claim she wanted a book to read to her father. It was the truth. He'd already grown restless from his forced confinement, and a book might be just the distraction he needed to alleviate his boredom.

Aye, that is what Sophronie would do.

She'd pick out two books. No doubt Papa would enjoy her reading to him in the afternoons, though she prayed the doctor would give his permission for her father to travel in a day or two. Overstaying their welcome could become most uncomfortable.

Somehow, she didn't think any of Waycross's female relatives—heavens, there were ten of them—would begrudge her a tome even if she had excused herself from joining the family for the midday meal and dinner. After all, as she told them, Papa had needed her. As instinctive nurturers, women had a better understanding of such matters, and Sophronie was confident none of the women she'd met this morning begrudged her taking care of her father.

Or so she told herself, feeling yet again the heat of scorching mortification flaming her cheeks when she recalled this morning's gaffe.

She and Waycross wedded, indeed.

Two more ill-suited people for matrimony had not walked the earth, in her opinion. What a colossal disaster such a union would be. The strife and contention would be intolerable.

The duke might very well take exception to her wandering his castle at night. Only, he'd been uncharacteristically polite these past two days. Rather than ease Sophronie's mind, his benevolence made her wary. Or perhaps she'd so long been accustomed to disliking and distrusting the man, she didn't know what to think when he wasn't being troublesome and obnoxious.

Waycross's interactions with his family were light, bantering, and astonishingly patient for the only male amongst a gaggle of energetic, slightly eccentric women. His grandmother's mistaken assumption that she'd overheard Sophronie and the duke were betrothed had certainly brought conversations to a tumbling halt.

Not a sound echoed in the dining room for a full five beats of Sophronie's hammering heart. Even the slack-jawed footman entering with fresh tea and the bug-eyed butler with a silver coffee pot in hand had gone still as Greek marble statues.

Mouth full of toast, Sophronie had frantically chewed while shaking her head, her gaze careening from one person to the other before crashing into the duke's.

Blue-gray eyes wide, his grace looked every bit as aghast as she felt at the absurd suggestion.

"Nae, Grandmother Larimore," he said with a good deal of vehemence and a trifle louder than even the hard-of-hearing woman required. "Miss Slater and I are *no'* affianced. We would no' suit. Besides, she is returnin' to America at the end of the month."

He'd turned a steely stare on his precocious aunts who'd caused the commotion—deliberately, Sophronie suspected. Both of their gazes held an unnerving, speculative gleam when they shifted them to Sophronie.

Surely they didn't think she was interested in becoming a duchess. Not any duchess, but the cantankerous Duke of Waycross's wife. A title held as much appeal to Sophronie as never seeing a horse again for as long as she lived. That would be hell on earth.

Praying that the floor would open and swallow her at breakfast had proved futile, so she'd resorted to the next best thing—avoiding Waycross. Naturally, she couldn't do that indefinitely—not in his home. Besides, she'd go stir crazy staying indoors now that Papa appeared to be on the mend.

Tomorrow, she'd ask Doctor Dargavel when her father could travel, and mayhap she'd go for a ride around the estate. She'd approach the duchess and ask her rather than disturb Waycross with such a trivial matter. If denied her request, Sophronie intended to take a long stroll. She'd also write and post several letters explaining their delay.

She turned her mind to the task of selecting a book.

"Now, what would Papa enjoy?"

Slowly walking alongside the brimming shelves, Sophronie couldn't help but be impressed. Tidy rows of books—many gold-embossed on their spines—filled the floor-to-ceiling bookcases. Two walls held ladders on rails which permitted one to climb to the upper shelves. An intricate spiral staircase wound its way upward to a miniature gallery, behind which perched a stunning round stained-glass window in shades of yellow, blue, and green.

With the silvery moonbeams as a celestial backdrop, the window was breathtaking and cast a luminescent glow over the quaint balcony.

That was where she'd read if it were her home.

"I'm betting the boring stuff is up high," she muttered to herself, craning her neck to look above her. "Or up there."

She shifted her attention to the balcony again.

She'd explore that treasure later if they remained at Balston House long enough for her to do so. Curiosity about the charming gallery and her desire to put Balston House and the Duke of Waycross behind her rooted around her middle, each vying for dominance.

Running a finger along the books' spines, she paused. "The history and evolution of horseshoes." Fascinating, but not calming. "No, something more relaxing for Papa, I think."

She settled on *The Vicar of Wakefield*.

"Now for me."

"I recommend *The Genteel Ladies' Guide to Practical Livin'*."

Gasping, Sophronie whipped around and, holding the book for her father against her chest with one hand and the candle in the air with the other, stared at the balcony's curved balustrade.

His shirt startling white in the muted light and unbuttoned, with the sleeves rolled to his elbows, the Duke of Waycross leaned over the railing. Moonlight bathed him in an iridescent glow, playing shadows across his craggy features.

Had he been watching her?

"Or," he continued, his tone riddled with jollity, *"The Gentlewoman's Companion; or a Guide to the Female Sex."* He held the book in his hand and squinted at the title, then lifting a candle she hadn't noticed until now, flicked open the cover and grinned.

Her tummy wobbled, as it had a disconcerting habit of doing whenever he smiled.

In a sonorous baritone, he intoned, *"Containin' Directions of Behavior, in all Places, Companies, Relations, and Conditions, from their Childhood down to Old Age."*

"Odious man," Sophronie muttered to herself.

How dare he insinuate she needed decorum lessons when he had been barely civil during most of their encounters?

"I think one of my sisters might've been readin' this, but I'm sure she wouldn't mind ye borrowin' it." He gave the book a doubtful glance.

"How...*resourceful* of you." Resourceful her bottom. "Nonetheless, I shall pass on the offer, Your Grace."

The light from the balcony she'd mistakenly believed was the full moon had been in fact a candle.

Although where he'd placed it, except upon the floor, to cause the light to splay out as it had was beyond her. Now she was all the more curious to investigate the charming area.

He snapped the book closed, set it aside, then descended the stairs. "I thought no'. It was published in 1673, and ye're much too modern a woman to adhere to such antiquated strictures. Ye canna even adhere to modern decorum."

The proverbial pot calling the kettle black.

Fashioning a falsely benign smile, Sophronie arched her eyebrows. "Perhaps there's a book on principles of politeness for peers, decorum for dukes, or a gentleman's guidelines for good manners *you* could peruse. Mayhap on one of these?"

She flicked a finger toward the nearby shelves.

Assuredly that sound that belonged to the night, filtering down to her wasn't a chuckle?

Casting a swift, wistful glance to the swollen shelves, where no doubt boring-as-plain-oatmeal-porridge books awaited her discovery, she resigned herself to the obvious. The opportunity to choose a book for herself had vanished. For tonight at least, she'd have to make do with the novel by Oliver Goldsmith she'd selected for Papa.

Sophronie's rude host had practically called her a hoyden. Rather than engage in another round of verbal sparring, she pivoted on her bare heels to leave. Arguing with the duke had become tiresome and predictable.

"I never took ye for a coward, Miss Slater." Waycross's boots snapped hard into the wood as he descended the last riser.

Coward?

He dared to call her a coward?

She who had dared to intrude upon men's domains on any number of occasions? She who had endured *le beau ton's* censorious whispers and haughty stares from the moment she'd arrived? She, who when out riding Cinnamon one day had defied two natives intent on stealing horses from the high grazing meadow? Those men had admired her fearlessness, declaring her sunset-threaded blonde hair gave her courage and boldness.

Gritting her teeth against the retort flying to her tongue, Sophronie slowly swiveled.

"*Coward?*"

Waycross had hit his target dead center, as she would bet her best gown he'd meant to.

One knee bent, he leaned against the shelves and crossed his arms. The posture emphasized his biceps and pulled the vee of his shirt wider, revealing a thatch of black, curly hair. Sheer brute strength warred with inbred, noble elegance. An arrogant smile teased one corner of his mouth, drawing her attention to the ebony stubble shadowing the lower part of his face.

"Ye're usin' yer father as a shield, lass."

The blighter was correct, but he was no gentleman for pointing it out.

She tossed her hair behind her. "Think what you will, but my father's recovery is my only priority, Your Grace."

He cocked his head, examining her through half-closed eyes from bare toes peeking inelegantly out from beneath her nightgown to her tousled hair hanging about her shoulders. Another ghost of a smile tipped that sculpted mouth.

"That's an interesting ensemble ye're wearin'."

Notching her chin upward an inch, she glared. "I forgot my nightrobe when I packed."

His lashed dubious raven brows together. "Ye packed yerself?"

"I do a great many things for myself, Your Grace. Although he is wealthy, my father believed I should be self-sufficient." Lifting a shoulder, she shifted the novel to under her arm. "Why should another do for me what I can do for myself?"

"Ye are provin' to be a more complex woman than I'd taken ye for, Miss Slater." The duke pushed away from the shelf and stalked forward until he stood almost toe to toe with her.

After his earlier insult, Sophronie stood her ground. Nevertheless, every instinct and the blood singing through her veins urged her to retreat. Never mind that she had to crane her neck to meet his piercing gaze or that his large form blocked the moonlight. She had never been called a coward in her life, and this boorish brute would not have the benefit of intimidating her.

"Most women are more complex than men give them credit for. I'd think you'd understand that given you live with ten of them. From my observation this morning, they are spirited, intelligent, remarkable women. Women I could admire very much had I time to become acquainted with them. Which I do not, because I intend to ask the doctor tomorrow if Papa is fit for travel."

The sooner her life returned to normal, the better. The sooner the Duke of Waycross was out of her life, the better too.

"I dinna think yer father is well enough to travel yet, lass." The duke flicked the collar of her jacket and a tiny thrill shot through her. "Ye'll have to endure my company for a few more days, Sophronie. If ye're brave enough to, that is."

He was so close she could smell his woodsy cologne, and her fingers itched to touch the tantalizing glimpse of chest hair his parted shirt revealed.

As much as Sophronie wanted to argue he was wrong, she suspected he was right. As an idea sprang to life, she grinned and took a step backward. "If you are correct and the doctor says we must delay a trifle longer, then I shall compete in the hunting course and use whatever prize money I win to pay for our stay here."

Instantly, she knew she'd said the wrong thing.

A thundercloud descended upon the duke's features, and he swore beneath his breath. The offended stare he fixed upon her actually raised her nape hair.

Upon realizing his financial reversals, guilt had assailed her that he'd been compelled to provide for two more mouths. Plus, the doctor hadn't breathed a word about a fee. Her actions had prevented the duke from buying one of the studs he'd wanted her father to inspect.

"I beg your pardon, Your Grace. I meant no offense, it's simply—"

"Ye are a guest in my home, Miss Slater. Ye insult me by suggestin' I would expect or accept compensation of any sort." He stomped to the door, then spun around to glare at her. "And ye will no' compete. Ye'll put dangerous, preposterous ideas into my sisters' heads which are already filled with frivolous nonsense and fanciful twaddle. I'll thank ye to keep yer radical American ideas and hoydenish behavior away from my family."

6

Balston House Stables

Early the next morning

Self-castigation whipped Evan's consciousness as he marched the path to the brick stables. The sun had barely crested the horizon, casting the land in dark purplish shadows and the sky in lavender, gold, coral, and heather-pink whisps.

He'd been unduly harsh with Miss Slater, but when she'd flippantly suggested she'd win the hunting course race and give him the prize money as payment for her and her father's stay, his temper had ignited faster than a flame to hay.

He clenched his jaw involuntarily in remembered ire.

She'd meant no harm…no real insult. But she'd struck a raw nerve. Every day, the burden of how he'd provide for his family if his horse breeding and racing ventures didn't flourish etched needle-like talons further into his already troubled mind.

For certain, he didn't need Miss Slater influencing his sisters with her wild, unconventional ways. Evan had a difficult enough time reining in his siblings on most days. He had no desire to crush their spirits, but neither did he want to deal with the commotions and chaos Miss Slater inevitably found herself right smack dab in the middle of.

Rubbing his nose as he angled toward the stable entrance, Evan calculated how soon the Slaters might leave. Given Doctor Dargavel's meticulous care, Evan would warrant not for another week. The physician wouldn't give his permission for George Slater to travel until he was positive the man's spleen and ribs were sufficiently healed to endure the jostling and bouncing over miles of rugged, rutted tracks to London.

Which meant Evan's precocious, vexing, maddening guest would be in Scotland for the

Wesleyans' outdoor fair the day after tomorrow.

He rolled his eyes heavenward in a silent bid for the Almighty's help and grace. Patience too, for that undoubtedly meant that the Slaters must be invited as his entire family always attended. It would be unconscionably rude to insist his uninvited guests remain at Balston House while he and his entourage of female relatives made a day of it partying with their friends and neighbors.

And yet…Evan was tempted as hell to do just that.

Every male instinct he possessed fairly screamed that Sophronie Slater was no more capable of resisting entering the hunting course race than the sun and moon could change positions in the cosmos.

She would enter.

Bloody tempest in a teapot.

Likely, she would win, and the somewhat orderly life he enjoyed would be turned head over arse for a goodly while.

Leah Wesleyan would not be pleased.

That almost made Evan smile.

Head down, contemplating the almost certain chaos

the next week portended, he entered the stables. His nostrils flared as the familiar scents of horses, hay, liniment, and feed created a tangy but not unpleasant mélange.

"You are a beauty, my friend," a female cooed softly.

Nae, not any female. Sophronie Slater's sophisticated Virginian drawl.

Evan halted in his tracks.

What in bloody hell was she doing in the stables before dawn? Especially when they'd been in the library together past midnight? Christ, even his grandmothers and aunts, all early risers, never left their comfortable mattresses before six.

"I wanted you for myself, but then I saw how you responded to the duke, and I knew you must be his." Clothing rustled as she moved about Eclipse's stall. "You will sire magnificent foals. I'm sorry that I shan't be here to see any of them, but I'll be far, far away, across an ocean."

Eclipse nickered.

"I know. We could've been friends too. But the

truth is, the duke needs you more than I do."

Something near chagrin heated Evan's face. Or mayhap it was something else. Something he couldn't identify.

The soothing sound of a brush moving rhythmically carried to Evan in the stable's early morning calm.

Was Sophronie brushing Eclipse?

Did she find the action as soothing as Evan did?

Evan glanced around the stables.

Where was McFarland? Kilburn? McArdle? *Anyone*?

Through the open doors on the other side of the stables, he caught sight of the three men, gazing into the pasture and enjoying a smoke. Evan didn't begrudge the servants stealing a few moments for themselves. All were hardworking and reliable. Besides, when Evan rode this early, he generally saddled his own mount.

Did they know Miss Slater had snuck into the stables?

The wench had probably given them a winsome smile, said something witty, and they'd let her have her way.

On silent feet, he approached Eclipse's stall. He watched Sophronie, small and fragile compared to the giant horse, skillfully brush the stallion, murmuring to the horse the whole while.

Eclipse spotted Evan first and, lifting his head, gave a snort of greeting.

Miss Slater stiffened before lifting her gaze to mesh with Evan's over the top of the stall gate. No guilt shone in her clear blue eyes for having trespassed in much the same manner as she had in the library last night.

She wore boy's clothing from tight breeches that delineated every feminine curve of her slender legs and nicely rounded bottom to a simple white shirt and the jacket she'd worn last night. Boots covered her legs to her knees, and she'd twisted her mane of hair into a simple knot atop her head. She was an aggravatingly appealing and perplexingly pretty combination of femininity and spitfire.

Evan rested his forearms on the top of the door. "What, pray tell, do ye think ye are doin?"

She stroked Eclipse's withers before pushing a curl that had sprung free of her haphazard chignon. "I was missing my horse, Cinnamon. Forgive me if I overstepped again."

Miss Sophronie Slater perpetually overstepped.

Eclipse gently nuzzled Evan's arm, and he obligingly rubbed between the horse's eyes. "Good mornin'. Ready for some exercise?"

A spark of wistfulness entered Miss Slater's gaze. She gave Eclipse one final pat and then approached the stall door. "I shall leave you to your ride, Your Grace."

Evan backed up a couple of paces and slid the door open.

"Would ye care to join me?"

He hadn't intended to ask Sophronie to ride with him, but he understood her need to be near horseflesh. To smell their scent, to feel their strong, sinewy bodies beneath you as you rode, to communicate with an animal that wasn't human.

Instant joy lit Miss Slater's face, causing her freckles to stand out in a rather adorable fashion. "You wouldn't mind?"

She replaced the brush on a nearby shelf, then wiped her hands on her breeches.

"I wouldn't have asked if I minded, Sophronie."

She digested that for a moment, then smiled. "I would, in truth. As long as I'm not intruding."

Evan shook his head and lifted a hand in greeting as his men wandered into the building. "Please saddle Starlight for Miss Slater."

"Aye, Yer Grace," Kilburn said, heading toward the mare's stall.

Nearly as black as Eclipse, but sporting a white patch on her forehead, Starlight was a spirited yet gentle mare. She was one of Evan's smaller horses and Larissa's favorite.

In short order, Evan and Miss Slater guided their mounts out of the barn and toward the circular drive. "Would ye like to see this year's foals?"

The foals were kept in a field on the other side of the castle.

"Do you need to ask, Yer Grace?" Grinning, Sophronie nodded. "Of course I would."

He chuckled. "I thought as much."

Evan kicked Eclipse's side, encouraging him into a canter.

Sophronie matched his pace, as comfortable in a saddle as any man Evan had seen.

"How fares yer father this mornin'?"

"He was still asleep when I slipped out. I thought I'd check on him before breakfast," she answered without looking at him.

They rode in companionable silence for several minutes. When they arrived at the pasture, Evan drew Eclipse to a stop, half-turned in his saddle, and pointed.

"Over there."

Five gangly foals nibbled the bright green grass, three frolicked about the meadow, and two played with each other as their tolerant mothers gazed on.

Sophronie sighed. "There's nothing I love more than horses, especially foals."

"Ye're actively involved with the breedin' process on yer father's estate?"

She gave him a considering, sidelong glance. "Not as much as you. I help select the stock and am always present for the births. Papa won't allow me to observe the actual process. He says it's not seeming for a lady."

Evan was in agreement. His female kin were never

permitted near the horseflesh when a stallion was being introduced to a broodmare.

"I think Papa forgets how many other animals we have on our plantation, Woodmead Hill." She presented her profile and studied the foals. "The act is not a mystery to me."

Evan nearly choked on a snort.

Not even his most outlandish grandmother or aunts spoke of animals coupling.

Sophronie, on the other hand, had stated the latter so matter-of-factly, she might've been conversing about the ocean's tides or how to bake scones. No bashful blushes, stammering, or downcast eyes. Sophronie Slater was the only female of Evan's acquaintance who could discuss such a delicate subject with ease.

He supposed he ought to be shocked or appalled, but he found her candidness refreshing.

"I'll race ye to the hill," Evan said on a sudden impulse, pointing to the mound a quarter-mile away.

Sophronie laughed and shook her head. "This little darling cannot hope to keep up with Eclipse. It would be most unfair. She may get her pride bruised."

Evan couldn't help but notice the way Sophronie's trim, muscled legs flexed as she expertly kept her seat upon the saddle.

He gave a sage nod. "Aye, I suspected ye'd be afraid of losin' to me."

"Afraid?" She scoffed, narrowing her eyes until only the irises showed. "If I win, you owe me an apology."

Eyebrows drawn together, Evan searched her flushed features and sparkling eyes. Why hadn't he ever noticed her beauty before? Probably because every time she opened her mouth, they clashed. Nonetheless, at this moment, suspended in time with the sun's newborn rays feathering her face in soft light and with the Highland meadow as a backdrop, Sophronie Slater was a heart-stopping vision.

Disturbed with the direction his wayward thoughts had taken him, Evan gave her a cocky grin. "For what?"

"Take your pick." She swirled a hand in the air near her ear. "There's been no shortage of offenses."

"What do I get if I win, lass?"

"You won't." In a trice, she kicked Starlight's

sides, and they bolted into motion.

Evan laughed, feeling younger and more carefree than he had in years. At one with the horse, Sophronie Slater rode like no woman he'd ever seen. Strength and litheness encapsulated in agile, graceful femininity. A juxtaposition of contrast and expectations.

"Ye cheated," he called, taking after her in hot pursuit. Eclipse could effortlessly overtake Starlight, but Evan found the chase every bit as exhilarating as the win.

Laughing, her strawberry blond hair slipped loose from its moorings and flowing behind her, Sophronie said something over her shoulder. Evan only caught part of what she shouted.

"…fair…love…war."

All's fair in love and war?

He let her keep a lead until they were within a few yards of their goal, and then he urged Eclipse past Starlight so that Evan won by a nose.

Eyes glittering, her face radiant, and her cheeks pink from exertion, Sophronie reined in her horse. She leaned forward and stroked Starlight's neck.

"Well done, my beauty. Well done."

A peculiar sensation tightened Evan's ribs and rooted around his heart.

As exasperating as Sophronie Slater was, she was, nevertheless, an enchanting paradox.

He guided Eclipse close enough that he could grasp a handful of her silky, fire-ribboned hair. He slowly wound it around his hand. "I won fairly, and now I'll claim my prize."

She blinked at him in surprise.

"But I didn't agree to give you a prize, Your Grace."

"Ah, but ye said all is fair in love and war."

Head cocked, he watched the parade of emotions flicker in her blue, blue eyes as he bent his head and brushed a featherlight, experimental kiss across her rosy lips.

Sophronie's mouth slackened, and she swayed toward him atop Starlight.

The essence of lilacs and lilies radiated off her creamy skin, causing Evan to wonder if she bathed in scented oil or with perfumed soap.

Head lifted, he peered into her eyes, so deeply and so intensely, he vowed his soul seared hers. "Which is it, lass? This aggravatin' thing, this perplexin' spark between us? Love or war?"

Gasping, Sophronie reared back as if struck. Eyes tumultuous, she pressed the back of her hand against her mouth before squaring her shoulders.

"Need you ask, Your Grace? It's always been war between us."

With that, she urged Starlight into a gallop back in the direction they'd come.

Evan remained where he was, watching Sophronie until the keep's imposing walls hid her from his view.

"I'm no' so sure about that anymore, lass. Nae at all."

Kirnochshire Manor
Wesleyans' Estate
12 August 1810

The sun shone high in the cloud-strewn afternoon sky as the coaches and riders from Balston House rounded the hedgerow-enclosed final bend in the Wesleyans' circular drive. All manner of conveyances paralleled the stone courtyard and were lined up in neat rows on a nearby green.

Evan's sisters had mentioned the annual fair was a popular event, but Sophronie had underestimated the number of attendees. She'd vow no fewer than one hundred conveyances dotted the grassland. Lord only knew how many additional guests had arrived by horseback as she had.

The smallest of Evan's sisters, Sarah, had generously offered Sophronie a soft kersey wool riding habit and hat the shade of new grass to wear. The fit was reasonably good, though a trifle long, and the color flattered her strawberry-blonde hair nicely. Sophronie would've preferred to have worn her breeches and jacket, but as the gathering was a Society event, she'd yielded to prudence and dressed accordingly.

Not for her sake, or even Papa's, but for Evan's sisters. They'd been the epitome of kindness to her, and for the first time in her life, she realized how very much she missed having siblings. And aunts and a mother and grandmothers. The women shared a relationship Sophronie had never had, nor would ever likely experience.

A dozen footmen in immaculate navy-blue and yellow livery descended from the manor house to assist the new arrivals. At once Sophronie recalled the stunning woman at Belleisle Racecourse. The menservants scurrying around and helping the guests wore the same distinguished livery as the men who'd followed the lady.

Papa, the Duchess of Waycross, and Evan's grandmothers alighted from the first coach. As he was still recovering, Papa leaned on a borrowed cane. She'd told him she needn't attend the fair, to which her father had chuckled and said he'd sooner receive another kick from a horse than deny her the enjoyment. When she'd protested that her father needn't accompany her, he'd insisted he was quite restored enough to lounge about in a chair for the day.

Skeptical of his readiness to be up and about, she'd secured a promise from him that if Doctor Dargavel said the outing was too strenuous this soon, Papa would consent and remain at Balston Manor to rest. To her surprise, the doctor had rubbed his chin then declared as long as Papa did not exert himself or engage in any physical activity more strenuous than lifting eating utensils or a wineglass, the outing was permissible.

Sophronie suspected the inactivity her father's recuperation required was taking a toll on him, but he also needed to realize how grave his injuries were. If he showed the slightest sign of tiring, they would promptly return to Balston House.

Evan's four aunts disembarked from the second coach as the footmen assisted Sophronie and Evan's sisters from their mounts.

Sophronie studied her father as he bent his neck to listen to something the Dowager Duchess of Waycross said. He looked so much improved if a trifle wan, especially around the eyes.

Sophronie would be right beside him to ensure that he wouldn't overdo it today. There'd be no racing for her either. More was the pity. Most especially after Evan's harsh invective for her to refrain from influencing his sisters with her *radical American ideas and hoydenish behavior.*

Papa smiled at her over the top of Lady Larimore's head, then winked. Her heart fairly sang in relief. She'd been so worried that he wouldn't recover or that his internal injuries were worse than the doctor had diagnosed. His presence here clearly indicated he was well on the road to a full recovery.

They might depart Scotland next week if he continued to improve.

Larissa looped her elbow through Sophronie's. "All of the activities are at the back of the house. I'm quite anticipatin' the archery event."

"As well ye should." Evan winked. "I'm wagerin' on the outcome."

Unlike several Scots parading about in kilts, he wore black pantaloons, a smoky gray jacket, and a tartan waistcoat. Rakishly dashing yet somber as always, Waycross kept drawing Sophronie's attention.

Eyes alight with excitement, Larissa flicked a glance over the assembled equipages.

"From the looks of it," she said, "it's a good turnout. That should make for an entertainin' afternoon. Last time, Thomasina McCurdy, who cannot see her hand before her face without her spectacles, shot an arrow into Lord Massingdale's ample backside. And Mr. Tedrow and Mr. Stanham, both soused to their eyeballs, engaged in a rousin' round of fisticuffs over the outcome of the boat race."

"Many Scots simply enjoy a good brawl." Evan cocked an eyebrow as he ran a hand over Eclipse's withers before the attentive footman led the horses away. "Some say it's in our blood."

"Indeed?" Sophronie slid him a side-eyed glance.

Was that why he was always ready to engage in verbal jousting with her?

"Come, Evan. Dinna be daft." Larissa gave him an incredulous look. "They argued over who was entitled to Miss Wesleyan's ribbon as the winner since they'd shared a rowboat."

Rosalind joined them and gave her brother a peeved glance. "I'm still miffed at ye, Evan, for forbiddin' any of us from enterin' the hunter's course." She lowered her attention to Sophronie and slid her mouth into a rather devilish sideways smile. "I would've enjoyed seein' ye beat that hoity-toity Miss Wesleyan, Sophronie."

Sophronie couldn't help but return the grin. "Please call me Roni. All of my closest friends do."

"Roni it is, then," Rosalind agreed with a wide grin. "Mother forbids us nicknames. She says if she'd wanted me to be called Rose, she would've named me Rose. I dinna ken how ye'd shorten Evan's, Sarah's, or Larissa's name in any event."

Sophronie's attention drifted to the duchess. She wasn't as imposing as many of the sophisticated English aristocrats Sophronie had met, but tall and handsome, there was no doubt she was a force to be reckoned with.

"How did ye come by yer pet name, Roni?" Sarah asked.

"I think my brother and sister called me Roni." Sophronie puzzled her forehead as she adjusted her leather riding gloves. "Papa says my full name was too difficult for them. Then after they and Mama died, Papa used it as a term of endearment and as a credit to their memories."

"How tragic, Roni," Rosalind put in. "Ye're an only child then, like Miss Wesleyan."

Sophronie's gaze drifted to the ostentatious house.

Was Leah Wesleyan the woman she'd seen at the racecourse?

"That's the only thing Roni has in common with Leah Wesleyan." Sarah pulled a face. "Roni is friendly, sincere, and kind, and she's no' stalkin' our brother for a husband."

"God forbid," Sophronie said a trifle too quickly,

which sent the sisters into peals of laughter and caused Evan to launch a raven brow high onto his forehead.

"We'd be at cross purposes constantly," she tried to explain, which only made his sisters giggle again and the planes of his face tighten. She'd offended him again, which only served to prove she was right.

He moved several feet away and gave her his back.

"Doth she protest too much?" Sarah teased good-naturedly.

No, I do not.

Sophronie had spent the past two days reliving that brief but delicious kiss. If she detested the Duke of Waycross as much as she'd convinced herself she did these past months, then why had his kiss left her breathless, confused, and utterly shattered?

Rather than her avoiding him as she had the first two days she'd been in residence at Balston House, Evan had been the one to make himself scarcer than a fat goose at Christmastide. His well-meaning family, attempting to assure Sophronie no slight was intended toward her, promised such behavior was not unusual for him.

Today's ride from Balston House to the Wesleyans' was the first time she'd seen him for more than a few minutes in passing. His manner was relaxed and jovial with his sisters but reserved and watchful with Sophronie.

Just as well. Sophronie was leaving in a week, and she didn't need to drag a complex, emotional tangle with her as extra baggage back to America. Whatever Evan mistakenly believed the *thing, the perplexing spark* between them was—it didn't exist.

She set aside her useless musings and focused on the current discussion.

"You don't care for Miss Wesleyan?" Sophronie had detected a distinct dislike for their hosts' daughter.

Sarah gave a most indelicate snort. "Leah Wesleyan's been after Evan worse than a dog after a flea." Her regard lingered on her brother. "She means to become the next Duchess of Waycross through fair means or foul, I suspect."

"Over my dead body," Rosalind muttered. "Or hers."

"Or Grandmother Gordonstone's." Larissa brushed

horsehair from the sleeve of her riding habit. "The last time she saw Miss Wesleyan, she told her she didn't fit the mold for a duchess, and Leah ought to set her cap for a gentleman other than Evan."

"Aye, and Leah laughed and pretended Grandmother was jestin'." Rosalind arched her eyebrows. "She wasna."

She exchanged a glance with her sisters that clearly said they objected to the union as fervently as she did.

"Isn't she suitable to be a duchess?" Sophronie couldn't explain the queer pull at her ribs that came with discussing a possible wife for Evan. Surely it was because his sisters obviously objected to such a match, which could only mean tension and trouble for the close-knit family later on.

Smiling, Eufamie McCollister claimed Sophronie's other arm. "That depends on what one considers suitable, my American friend. Miss Wesleyan is beautiful, has impeccable manners, never raises her voice or says anythin' untoward, dresses like a queen, and yet, an asp in the dead of winter possesses more warmth and benevolence."

"Speak of the devil's handmaiden," Rosalind whispered out the side of her mouth, her attention fixed behind Sophronie.

Sophronie knew before she turned and faced the stairs ascending to the manor who she'd see standing there. The striking woman she'd seen at the racecourse in the vibrant red and black riding habit lingered at the top of the stair. Today, she was gorgeous in sapphire blue.

As those confident of their power and position often do, she affected various poses to show off her exquisite riding habit and even more exquisite figure. She was, in a word, breathtaking from her intricately coiffed ebony hair to her ruby-red lips.

This was a woman who knew what she wanted and was seldom denied anything.

"Good afternoon, Your Grace," Leah Wesleyan said in practiced sultry tones. "How nice that your entire family—*and American guests*—could attend our little soiree today."

Rather than the lilting brogue Evan's female kin preferred, Miss Wesleyan spoke the king's clipped English, and Sophronie had to strain her ears to detect even the slightest hint of a burr. However, even a deaf man could've detected the distinct frigidness in her tenor when she mentioned Evan's guests.

Perhaps he'd been mistaken regarding Sophronie's and Papa's welcome despite having assured both of them that as Evan's house guests, the invitation extended to them as well.

Miss Wesleyan descended the steps and extended one black-gloved hand toward the duke. Evan obligingly kissed her hand. "Miss Wesleyan. I look forward to an invigoratin' afternoon."

"As do I, Your Grace." She practically purred in feline satisfaction as she snagged his arm and sidled up to him. She took Sophronie's measure from her borrowed hat to her halfboots before gravitating her arctic regard to Evan's sisters and other female relatives.

There was no love lost between them, and in fact, Sophronie detected a distinct glint of animosity in Miss Wesleyan's cold blue eyes. A shudder scuttled from Sophronie's waist to her nape when the woman turned her shrewd gaze upon her once more.

The dislike was instant, powerful, and wholly mutual.

Sophronie couldn't fathom Evan marrying a woman who so blatantly disliked his family. He'd always be caught in the middle, trying to pacify his wife and appease his mother, aunts, sisters, and the rest. He'd never know a moment's peace or contentment.

"I swear if Evan marries that she-cat, I'm off to live in a crofter's cottage, roofless or no'," grumbled Rosalind.

Her expression troubled, Sarah rolled a shoulder. "If he does wed her, she'll make our lives hell, but Evan mustn't know we feel this way. He carries enough burden. We'll just have to pray harder that the Good Lord brings him a kind wife. Someone who fits in with our family."

She took in her sisters' grim features and Sophronie's dubious look.

"It's possible," Sarah defended.

"Let me introduce ye to George and Sophronie Slater, Miss Wesleyan," Evan said.

At once, Sophronie sought out her father. He was already nearly upon them, and as if sensing Sophronie's unease, gave her a reassuring smile. Strain etched fine lines at the outer corners of his eyes. She had the unsettling feeling he'd pushed himself too early.

A brittle smile curving her rouged lips, Miss Wesleyan glided across the courtyard. Evan made the introductions, to which Miss Wesleyan responded with a glacial nod. In short order, everyone headed toward the festivities, Evan and their hosts' daughter in the lead.

As they strolled toward the green and tents, Miss Wesleyan kept up a steady stream of conversation with Evan and pointedly ignored everyone else.

"Miss Slater?" the Dowager Duchess of Waycross called as she leaned upon her cane.

Sophronie slowed her pace and waited for the lady. "Yes, Your Grace?"

"Please do tell me that ye are to attempt the hunter's course today." She slid Miss Wesleyan a sly, not entirely friendly glance. "Evan assures me ye are capable of winnin'."

Had he indeed?

Precisely when had that fascinating conversation taken place?

Sophronie followed the dowager's stare to find Miss Wesleyan and Evan had stopped. The young woman studied Sophronie with disturbing, spine-tingling intent.

Rarely did Sophronie have a forceful aversion to someone on sight. In truth, she couldn't recall the phenomenon having ever happened before. But as God was her witness, her very spirit rebelled at being near Miss Wesleyan.

"I ken ye are an accomplished horsewoman and have won many a race." The dowager bobbed her head toward Lady Larimore. "What say ye, Canne? Can our Miss Slater take the prize today?"

Lady Larimore swung her gaze between the dowager, Miss Wesleyan, and Sophronie twice before a slow grin spread across her wrinkled face.

Oh, you wicked, wicked tabbies.

Sophronie knew precisely what they were up to. They were making a May game of Miss Wesleyan and having a bit of fun at Sophronie's expense too.

"Why, Lizabeth, I dinna ken. Evan, is yer American competin'?" Lady Larimore asked with false guilelessness. "I may break my own rule and wager on the outcome if she is."

"Aye, me as well, Canne." A smile wreathed the

dowager's wrinkled face, pleating it like the folds of a fan. "Sure things are so rare, I'd be a numpty no' to, ye ken."

Miss Wesleyan's eyes shrank into shrewd slits as she raked her antagonistic gaze over Sophronie.

"*You* race, Miss Slater?" she asked with such haughty disdain and exaggerated disbelief, she might've asked if Sophronie bathed regularly.

"I do." Let the banshee make of that what she would.

"Odd." Miss Wesleyan puzzled her brow in exaggerated confusion. "I don't recall seeing your name on the entry form. Or perhaps hunter's courses in America are not as taxing as those in Scotland, and you were afraid to give it a go?" Her curved lips slid into a serpent's deceitful smile. "Completely understandable."

Sophronie tipped her head at a fiercely whispered expletive to her right but forced herself not to look in that direction.

One of Evan's relatives had called Miss Wesleyan a bitch.

Evan's strong jaw repeatedly flexed with his

undisguised irritation as he cut a glance toward the festivities. He did not want Sophronie to race today. He'd made that abundantly clear the other night, and she didn't intend to give him further reason to disapprove of her.

She could race until her heart was content once she was back home in Virginia.

"Jealous harridan," one of the sisters or aunts murmured beneath her breath.

"Hush," another shushed her.

Papa had come to a standstill as well, and the attention of everyone in their entourage shifted from Miss Wesleyan to Sophronie.

Evan had yet to answer his grandmother.

Sophronie, who never let another woman's spitefulness get beneath her skin, itched to slap the smug expression from Leah Wesleyan's beautiful face. She knew precisely what she was doing, despite her wide innocent eyes and soft, cultured tone.

"Regrettably, my daughter is here merely as an observer today, Lady Larimore." Papa addressed Evan's grandmother, rather than the haughty heiress. "You are aware that I am recovering from an accident, and I'd prefer Sophronie to remain near me."

He gave Sophronie one of his do-not-argue-with-me looks.

"Of course, Mr. Slater." Lady Larimore had the good grace to appear genuinely abashed.

Miss Wesleyan laughed, a humorless tinkle that held no warmth. "How gallant of you, Mr. Slater, to come to your daughter's defense and protect her from a humiliating experience." She angled her dainty chin upward. "I've won the women's hunter's course for the past five years."

"Only because we're no' allowed to compete, ye dimwitted ninny."

Sophronie didn't need to look to know Rosalind had made that declaration, followed by a pained whoof as someone likely elbowed her in the side.

Miss Wesleyan turned her face up to Evan and offered a sincere smile. Well, as sincere as an alligator with its prey in its beady sights could. "What do you say, Evan? Shall your American guest add her name to the women's course even though the outcome is predetermined?"

Evan's gaze landed on Sophronie, and there was a question in his blue-gray eyes.

He would let her race if she wanted to after all.

She could see that truth in the way the corners of his eyes flexed the merest bit. Her heart swelled with emotion. He'd put aside his declaration and desire that she couldn't compete because Miss Wesleyan was behaving like a spiteful twit.

Sophronie lifted her chin in silent assent, and Evan grinned.

"Nae, Miss Wesleyan." He adjusted his hat, his eyes bright with hilarity. "Miss Slater will no' compete in the women's course."

"I thought not." Miss Wesleyan preened in smug satisfaction, practically rubbing herself on Evan's arm.

He disentangled himself from her tentacles and, disregarding her petulant glower, took the few steps to where Sophronie stood. Tucking her hand into his elbow, he passed his gaze over everyone.

"If Miss Slater chooses to race today, she'll compete against the men, astride Eclipse."

8

Kirnochshire Manor
Hunter's Race Course
Three hours later

*G*od's teeth.

Evan still couldn't fathom what bloody, maggoty impulse had prompted him to declare that Sophronie would ride Eclipse. Something potent and uncontrollable had welled up inside him at Leah's deliberately targeting Sophronie—attempting to draw blood with her cutting wit and double-edged words.

The impulse to protect Sophronie, though he knew full well she didn't need, want, or appreciate the gesture, had overcome him. Nae, the urge to firmly put Leah in her place had motivated him equally as much.

For all of her pretentiousness, Leah Wesleyan would never toss Society's strictures aside and ride astride, let alone compete with the men. Evan had no doubt Sophronie could manage the course atop Eclipse. Still, he'd also made her the object of speculation and perhaps additional scorn by declaring she'd enter the gentleman's race.

Stupid, stupid fool.

Only Sophronie Slater could make him completely forget himself.

"Evan, I don't have to race." The breeze caught a wisp of her rose-gold hair and teased her temple. "It is of no import to me."

It wasn't.

Her sincerity wasn't an act. She honestly didn't care what people thought of her, and it was so refreshing and unexpectedly welcome that an unidentifiable emotion battered the walls of his chest.

That this woman, this firebrand who barely reached his shoulder, should have such an impact on him befuddled and bemused him. Why she, of all women, had the power to do so was equally confounding.

They stood a few feet away from the men preparing themselves for the upcoming competition in the shade of an oak grove. Several cast her speculative or sardonic glances.

Sophronie was either accomplished at ignoring the searing looks sent her way, or she honestly hadn't noticed.

Earnestness etched upon her pretty features, she touched his forearm. "I have nothing to prove, and I don't care what Miss Wesleyan or any of the others think of me. I'm leaving Scotland in a few days and will never see any of them again anyway."

"Aye, lass, I ken ye dinna care. But I do."

Evan shouldn't care a whit that Sophronie's name was on every tongue thanks to him, but he did. Much more than he ought to and assuredly more than was wise. Besides, the truth of it was, Evan would thoroughly enjoy watching her compete. Never had he met a woman more at home in the saddle, and what was more, he sincerely believed she could win.

He scrubbed a hand through his hair.

Regardless, the day wasn't a total loss.

The past few minutes had convinced him of one thing—Leah Wesleyan would never become the next Duchess of Waycross, even if she was an heiress and a match between their families would substantially enlarge the duchy's holdings.

Her temperament and personality rubbed Evan raw, and he had observed her unkindness toward his family too many times. Though her father wasn't titled, she behaved as if his family were inferior to hers—even to the point of scorning his family's brogue.

More than once, her condescending and patronizing attitude toward his kin had gravitated to waspishness and criticism. She'd even hinted that Balston House was too small for so many of his relatives. The keep boasted two-and twenty bedchambers. The plain unadulterated truth of it was, she didn't want any other females vying for his attention or undermining her absolute control.

The fact that another woman, this one not even a relative, now resided under the same roof as Evan had Leah seething with envy. Slightly panicking too, since Evan couldn't hide his admiration of Sophronie when it came to her knowledge of horseflesh or her riding ability.

Leah had always been selfish and self-centered. As an only child, she'd been cosseted and pampered. Coincidentally, so had Sophronie Slater. While both women possessed strong personalities and inherent confidence, Leah was conceited, self-important, and believed herself superior to nearly everyone.

Sophronie, on the other hand, accepted others, and he'd never heard her disparage anyone. Not even those who had been less than gracious to her in England. There had been many who'd mocked her accent, found fault with her mannerisms, took exception to her freckles and lack of artifice, and disdained her simply because she was an American.

"Yer father is none too pleased with me." Evan jutted his chin toward George Slater.

"He'll forgive you. He doesn't hold grudges."

Sophronie half-turned to search out her father and Evan's mother and grandmothers sitting beneath one of the large white tents. They shared a table, sipped cool beverages, and nibbled on the heaping plates of tantalizing foods expressionless footmen had served them. Slater looked a bit more ashen than he had when they'd arrived.

Was that due to his annoyance with Sophronie and Evan, or should he have stayed abed a while longer?

As it had since he'd sat down, Slater's focus remained on Evan and Sophronie.

"He wants me to be ladylike, though I fear it's a lost cause." She shrugged, and a rueful smile tipped her mouth upward, making her appear vulnerable. In this light, the smattering of freckles stood out upon her delicate face. "I think he feels like he's failed as a father because I'm not—because I seldom fit in, and I'm a hoyden."

Evan made a sound in his throat as her unintended barb hit home with infallible accuracy.

He'd called her that very thing.

That night in the library, beset with worries, Evan had lashed out unfairly, his stress eclipsing his good manners and common sense. He ran his regard over Sophronie, from her expressive eyes that gave away nearly everything she was thinking, to the slightly stubborn tulip of a chin and her plump, perpetually smiling mouth.

There were ladies, and then there were *ladies*.

"I dinna think because ye wear breeches and ride astride ye are no' a lady."

He scrutinized the crowd of nearly two hundred milling about the lawns. There were many present today who considered themselves ladies that he did not.

"Ho there, Waycross. Heard ye've been stirrin' up a wee bit of trouble." A teasing grin framing his face, Tobias Forsythe, Duke of Heatherston, approached. His keen blue gaze roved over Sophronie as she turned to face him. "So this is the lass everyone is speakin' of? She'll race with the men?"

"Aye, Heatherston, she is. If she's willin'."

"She's a wee sprite of a thing, Evan." Skeptical lines furrowed Heatherston's forehead.

"She can do it. I'd wager Balston House on it."

"*She's* standing right here and can hear everything you are saying about her," Sophronie interjected with a wry upward sweep of her lips and hands planted on her hips.

Evan and Heatherston exchanged a glance at the

spitfire taking them to task.

She shook her finger. "You'd be a fool to make such a wager, Evan. There is never any guarantee of the outcome of an obstacle course race. There are too many unknowns for anyone to wisely wager more than a small amount they can afford to lose."

"Och, the lass is as intelligent and wise as she is lovely." Giving Evan a wicked grin, Heatherston swept Sophronie a bow. "I believe we attended the same Christmastide house party, Miss Slater."

"We did indeed, Your Grace." She dipped a shallow curtsy. "Are you competing today?"

"Alas, I did no' enter this year." He replaced his hat and swept his gaze over the assembling competitors. "My mount strained a fetlock, and I willna ride another."

Sophronie nodded, that little wisp of hair brushing her temple again. "I understand completely. I prefer to ride my horse, but she's in Virginia. She knows me so well, and I her, that it's almost as if we become one being when I'm atop her. I miss her dreadfully."

"The lass sounds exactly like ye, Waycross, when

ye speak of horseflesh." Chuckling, Heatherston folded his arms, no small amount of speculation in his keen gaze as he looked between Evan and Sophronie.

"Admirin' and respectin' equines is a unifying bond across all mankind dating back thousands of years," Evan offered lamely, even as his ears turned hot.

Damn, Heatherston.

He had Evan blushing like a wet-behind-the-ears pup.

Why did everyone keep on insinuating a match between Sophronie and him would be ideal? There was much more to the marriage union than a passion for horses. Being able to refrain from arguing for more than half an hour, for instance.

Sophronie caught Evan's eye. "We don't have anything in common other than our love of horses."

"Och, well, many *friendships* have been forged on far less." Heatherston's eyes lit with hilarity.

He was deliberately goading Evan—God rot the bounder.

"Indeed," Evan drawled.

"What's it to be then, Miss Slater?" Heatherston

jerked his chin toward the other riders. "Will ye prove that a woman can do anythin' a man can?"

Sophronie's focus shifted to the men, many of whom regarded her with hostility. Her expression remained benign, but a shadow dimmed her vibrant eyes for a second.

"I wouldn't think a man of your station would embrace that progressive ideal, Your Grace. Besides, I don't believe women can or should do everything a man does. I do believe, however, that women should be permitted to try if they so desire."

"Well said, Miss Slater." Heatherston clapped his hands together then slapped Evan on the shoulder. "I'm headed back to London next week. Let's arrange to get together before then, shall we?"

"Absolutely," Evan agreed. "Come for dinner Friday. I'll let Mother ken."

"Sophronie. Roni!"

The three of them turned as one to see Sarah and Larissa hurrying across the green.

At once, Evan searched the tent where his mother, grandmothers, and Slater had been reposing a few minutes before. Other guests had taken up residence at their table, and there was no sign of them.

Features sober and pallid beneath their bonnets, his sisters, both quite out of breath, stumbled to a halt.

"Ye must come at once, Roni." Sarah took Sophronie's hand. "Yer father collapsed."

"Mother and Grandmother are with him," Larissa said on the verge of tears.

Every vestige of color drained from Sophronie's face, and she swayed.

"Steady now, lass." Evan put his arm around her. "I'm here. All will be well."

Or would it?

Evan hadn't been happy with Slater's decision to attend the fair today, but who was he to argue with the physician?

"What happened?" Worry rendered Sophronie's voice husky.

"We dinna ken," Sarah said. "Miss Wesleyan says she found him on the other side of the house."

"Alone? That makes no sense." Face crumpled with worry, Sophronie shook her head. "Why would he have been there?"

Evan turned her toward the entrance. "We'll sort all of that out later. For now, let's find yer father and assess the situation."

From his sisters' expression, Slater's condition must be grave indeed.

"What can I do?" Heatherston asked, falling into step beside Evan.

"Send for Doctor Dargavel, and have him meet us at Balston House." Evan guided Sophronie forward, aware of the guests' curious gazes boring into them. "Have my coach readied too, please."

"At once. I'll take a raincheck on that dinner invitation, my friend." Heatherston set off at a brisk pace, effectively dodging questions from intrusive guests.

"Please God," Sophronie whispered as she clutched Evan's arm.

He glanced downward to see her eyes squeezed shut.

"Please don't take my father from me. He is all I have in this world."

9

Balston House

Outside George Slater's bedchamber

Hands clenched and chin tucked to her chest, Sophronie paced outside her father's bedchamber.

The doctor had arrived soon after they'd returned from the Wesleyans', and Papa had been tucked into bed. After ushering everyone from her father's chamber, he'd closed the door with a firm, final-sounding snick.

One. Two. Three. Four. Five.

She stepped on the flowers in the Aubusson carpet as she marched one direction, then pivoted and made the return journey, once more treading on the festive red blossoms.

Though no more than ten or fifteen minutes had passed since the physician had shooed them from the room, each second stretched out endlessly as Sophronie's mind ran rampant with all manner of imaginings.

What had happened?

Why on earth had her father been on that side of the house and away from the rest of the guests?

What would she do if Papa died?

What was taking the physician so dang-fangled long?

Evan leaned a shoulder against the wall beside her father's bedroom door and silently watched her sojourn up and back. Up and back. Up and back.

The rest of his family had retired to the chapel to pray.

He hadn't been exaggerating when he said his womenfolk were praying people.

"I'll ask for a light repast to be kept at the ready. Sandwiches, fruit, cold meats, and cheese. Tea and sherry too. It may be a long night," the duchess had announced before giving Sophronie a warm hug and a kiss on the cheek. "I am here if ye need me, my dear."

Sophronie was at once grateful and petrified at the possible implication of her kind words. She stopped and stared at the closed door, willing it to open and the physician to come out and tell her all was well. That her father had simply overestimated his strength and ability to venture out.

With each passing minute, that hope faded until, with every heartbeat, a voice in her head repeated.

Papa's going to die.

Papa's going to die.

Papa's going to die.

A desperate sound escaped her lips, and she bit the inside of her cheek to still the hysteria bubbling under the surface of her hard-won composure.

Evan straightened and came to her side. He faced the door and rocked back onto his heels.

"I would spare ye this worry."

She glanced upward for a moment, then returned her focus to the door, incapable of getting words past the lump in her tight throat. Instead, she nodded. Evan's presence was comforting, and Sophronie wanted to wrap her arms around his waist and bury her face in his chest.

People always said how strong she was. They were wrong. It was a veneer, a charade, a wall to protect herself. She wasn't strong. She had fears and worries just like everyone else. She simply hid hers behind a bright smile, daring behavior, and a resilient spirit.

"I shouldn't have gone." Her voice cracked, and she swallowed. "If I hadn't gone to the Wesleyans', Papa wouldn't have either. My selfishness caused this. Once more my actions have brought calamity upon my father."

"Nae, Sophronie."

Evan turned her into his arms, and then she was against the solid wall of his chest as she'd yearned to be, absorbing his strength and the woodsy, musky scent of his cologne. He was her rock at this moment, and she clung to him.

"Ye canna blame yerself, lass," he murmured into her hair.

I can and do.

"Unfortunate things happen in life," Evan said.

"It's human nature to want to find a cause, a reason, someone to blame. But the truth of it is, lass, more often than no', what happens is out of our control."

His heart beat a steady, comforting rhythm beneath her ear.

"We can choose to fight what comes our way, Sophronie, become angry and bitter, or acknowledge that a higher, wiser force is at work. My Grandmother Gordonstone says that all things work for good for them that love the Lord."

"Do you believe that?" she asked through her clogged throat.

"Honestly, I dinna ken." Evan rested his chin upon Sophronie's head. "I've seen the wicked prevail while the innocent are cheated. I dinna understand why some people die and others live. Why some prosper and others dinna. 'Tis a great riddle to be sure, and I dinna pretend to have the answer."

Tears crept from the corners of Sophronie's eyes, and she burrowed deeper into his chest, accepting the comfort he offered. This man who she'd considered her nemesis murmured soothing words and ran his big hands over her shoulders and back.

There was nothing the least sexual or inappropriate in his touch. With many females in his household, he'd likely had a great deal of practice at this sort of thing. Eyes closed, she stood there, accepting the comfort he offered. He'd become a steadying force in her life this past week.

At long last, the door opened, and they stepped apart. Sophronie wiped her eyes with her fingertips and gazed at the doctor expectantly.

He gave her a tired, benevolent smile. "Yer father has asked me to wait to speak with ye, Miss Slater, until after he has spoken with his grace."

"But why?" Her gaze flew to the narrow opening between the door and the doorframe.

"He'll explain his reasons to ye himself, lass," Doctor Dargavel said. "Yer Grace, Mr. Slater awaits ye."

With a slight nod, and an apologetic glance to Sophronie, Evan slipped through the doorway and shut the door behind him.

"Lass, excuse me while I attend to a few issues for

yer father. I'll return in a few minutes and apprise ye of everythin'." He patted her shoulder in a fatherly fashion. "Ye should eat somethin'."

"I cannot." The idea of eating anything made her want to vomit.

She watched him until he rounded the corner farther along the corridor.

Why had Papa asked to see the duke before her?

Evan stood beside George Slater's bed. He'd seen dying men before, and there was no doubt that life was rapidly fading from Sophronie's father. He pulled a chair near the bed then sat.

"Mr. Slater, ye wished to speak with me?"

For several moments, the only sign of life in the ghostly white man was the gentle rising and falling of Slater's chest. Evan shifted in the chair. If he didn't miss his mark, Slater wouldn't last the night, and Sophronie must say her goodbyes soon.

How awful to lose her father when they were so far

from the comforts of home.

"Mr. Slater?" Evan tentatively touched the man's shoulder with his forefinger.

Slowly, as if it took supreme effort, Slater's eyelids crept open. He offered a weak smile.

"Your Grace."

Evan waved the honorific away. "Evan, please."

"Water," Slater croaked.

Evan gently propped him up, then put the glass of water that had been sitting on the nightstand to the man's mouth.

Slater took a couple of shallow swallows before turning his head away.

Evan lowered him to the plump pillows once more.

"I want you to marry Sophronie," Slater whispered without preamble.

Evan froze in putting the glass down. "I beg yer pardon?"

"I'm dying. I shan't deceive myself. Roni has no kin in America. Few friends either." Slater reached for Evan's hand. "I shall bequeath you half of my estate, including my horses, if you marry her. The other half is hers to do with as she wishes."

Slater was a wealthy man. Exceedingly wealthy. It was vulgar to discuss such things in polite company, but people still talked. He'd invested in several successful ventures while in England too.

"Why me?" Evan loosened his neckcloth, practically gulping for air. The room suddenly felt too confined, and he couldn't draw enough air into his lungs. "She canna abide me."

The idea was absurd. Preposterous. Ludicrous.

It bordered on insane, in point of fact.

Had Slater hit his head when he fell?

"I dinna understand why ye are askin' this of me, George." Evan raked a hand through his hair. "Dinna ye want yer daughter happy?"

"I don't trust any other man to take care of her or to honor my wishes. Too many men only care for her fortune. She's unique, a wildflower amongst carefully tended blooms. She needs a man who won't try to tame her wild ways."

Evan granted him that slice of truth.

But he was not that man. He wasn't ready to marry

for wealth yet. He wasn't that desperate.

Slater closed his eyes for several heartbeats, and just when Evan thought he'd fallen asleep, they popped open again. "Sophronie's strong-willed and unconventional, Evan, but you already know that. Regardless, I've seen how she responds to you."

Evan knew all too well how she responded to him. Usually piss and vinegar, though of late, there had been a pleasant moment or two. Their all-too-brief kiss had been very pleasant indeed.

The urge to vehemently deny George Slater's last wish was on the tip of Evan's tongue.

No. No. Bloody hell, no.

Slater studied Evan's face intensely for an uncomfortably long measure. "Love and hate are opposite sides of the same coin, my boy. There is something between the two of you. Besides, you raise and race horseflesh. That alone will go a long way toward her happiness and contentment. You would do well to heed her advice on those matters. She, not me, is the reason our stables are as successful as they are."

Evan flopped back into the chair, and it squeaked a

protest at the rough treatment.

Half of Slater's estate would pay off all of his debts, enable him to dower his sisters, allow him to buy prime breeding stock, and still have a fortune to make the improvements he'd longed to implement on his various properties. Hell, he could probably survive on the interest alone, and then there was the man's many investments.

This was a wholly unexpected gift from heaven.

Except for one petite, blue-eyed, gold-and-fire-haired detail.

Sophronie would never agree to it. Never.

"What say you, Evan? Will you marry my daughter and allow me to rest in peace knowing she'll be well cared for and that no philandering rascal will swindle her out of her money or abuse her?"

This opportunity was a miraculous answer to prayer.

Evan could do far worse for a bride than Sophronie Slater.

Leah Wesleyan's beautiful face came into view.

Aye, far, far worse.

God curse him for a fool. Evan would do it and pray he wasn't making the worst mistake of his life. He sighed and, leaning forward, rested his elbows on his knees. "If Sophronie agrees, I do as well."

"Tonight, so that I can bear witness?"

Tonight? Bloody hell.

Slater shifted and groaned. "I've asked the doctor to send for a cleric and a solicitor. I know my time grows short."

What exactly was he dying from?

An internal injury was Evan's best guess.

"Aye," he reluctantly acquiesced. "Tonight, but only if Sophronie is completely willin'. I willna have her forced. It must be her free choice."

A marriage of convenience was distasteful, but a forced marriage was repugnant. Evan would have no part in manipulating Sophronie, no matter how much wealth he was offered.

"She's a good girl—a loving daughter. She'll grant…my last request." Slater's eyes drifted shut, and he slept.

"I wouldna bet my life on that."

10

Unable to bear waiting any longer, Sophronie silently opened the door to her father's chamber and peeked inside. Head in his hands and shoulders slumped as if the weight he bore upon those broad shoulders was too much to bear, Evan sat beside her father's bed.

A long, slow, agonized hiss escaped her, drawing Evan's attention.

He raised his head, sorrow and another unidentifiable emotion etched upon his rugged features.

Almost against her will, she gravitated her focus to her father's ghastly white face. Never had he looked so frail and vulnerable. The large bed seemed to swallow him, and he was so very, unnaturally still.

"Is he…?" Every muscle in her body went rigid as she braced herself for the worst. Swallowing against the dread pummeling her insides, she took two tentative paces into the room. "Is he dead?"

"Nae, lass." Evan rose at once and crossed to her. He touched her shoulder and gave a reassuring squeeze. "He's merely sleepin'."

"You're certain?" Her agitated gaze clashed with his troubled one before drifting to her insensate father again. "Why is he so white, Evan?" she whispered past stiff lips. "It's as if all of the blood has drained from him."

She feared she mightn't be far off the mark.

Where was the doctor?

He said he'd only be a few minutes.

He should be here to answer the questions tormenting her.

Likely he'd stopped off in the kitchen for a scone and marmalade again. The uncharitable thought had her glancing at the gaping doorway in search of the physician.

"I dinna ken, Sophronie. The doctor will tell ye what he kens when he returns."

"*When* he returns." She pressed her lips together.

"He should be here with Papa," she whispered fiercely. "What could possibly be more important than that right now?"

Rather than answer her, Evan gently took her elbow. "Come, sit down."

She didn't resist but allowed him to lead her to the chair he'd just vacated.

Slightly unsteady, Sophronie sank onto the seat. Still wearing the borrowed riding habit, she held a hand to her forehead. The gesture did nothing to calm her ricocheting thoughts or the disjointed thumping of her heart. "I know I'm overstepping, but what did Papa say to you? What was so important that he must speak to you before me?"

She glanced upward, fully aware her voice held a pleading note, and hurt punctuated her tone.

Evan rubbed two fingers over an eyebrow, an apology in his reluctant blue-gray eyes.

"Forgive me, Sophronie, but it's no' for me to say."

Sophronie scowled, frustration and fear tightening the tangled knot in the pit of her stomach. She inhaled a large breath, her chest expanding with the movement, and took her father's hand.

"He's dying, isn't he?" There was no point in equivocating.

Evan paused for several heartbeats, then released a raspy sigh. "I believe so, but we must wait for the doctor to tell us as much."

Oddly calm and surprisingly composed, she nodded. Sophronie had never been the sort for histrionics and dramatics, though if there ever were a time for either, sitting beside her dying father's bedside qualified.

"I wish I had a large family as you do, Evan. It wouldn't make Papa's passing any easier, but at least I'd have other loving relatives around me to ease the pain." Feeling somewhat dazed and struggling to focus and grasp the reality of this awful moment, she stared across the room. "There's no one in Virginia except for a few friends."

She'd make the return voyage by herself now. How could she possibly pick up the life she'd left months ago by herself? Tears blurred her vision, and she kissed her father's hand.

"Please don't leave me, Papa. I need you."

It didn't matter that Evan heard her pleas. All that mattered was the man who'd kept her safe, who'd loved her unconditionally despite her mulishness and rebellious tendencies, would be no more.

Pain clamped her heart, and she struggled to breathe. Guilt brutally kicked her in the ribs as well. Despite Evan's kind reassurances of a few days ago, she couldn't help but blame herself.

Closing her eyes, she prayed. *God, if you let my father live, I vow I'll never be impetuous or imprudent again. I'll behave with perfect decorum and never give Papa cause to be troubled or ashamed of my behavior.*

Sophronie opened her eyes to find Evan studying her.

Doctor Dargavel trundled in. He twisted his mouth into a semblance of benevolent smile for Sophronie as he lifted her father's wrist and felt for a pulse. "Weak, but steady."

He looked to Evan. "I've done as he instructed."

All at once, Sophronie had had enough, and her control snapped. "Why am I, his daughter, the only one uninformed? What, pray tell, did my father say to you, Evan?" She pinned the doctor with an accusatory gaze. "And why haven't you informed me, his next of kin, of his condition, but instead are running errands for him?"

The doctor grasped his lapels and eyed her. "My duty is always to my patient, lass. Yer father asked to speak with his grace, no' ye, first. He also asked me to perform a couple of tasks to ease his mind and his passin'."

His passing.

Oh, God.

There it was. Out in the open, straight from the physician's mouth. Pain such as she'd never known cleaved her in two. How she remained upright she couldn't fathom.

Feeling at once utterly selfish and like a harridan and horrible daughter, Sophronie lowered her eyes to her lap and nodded. "Of course," she whispered. "I apologize."

"Sophronie? Is that you?"

She perked up and leaned forward. "Yes, Papa. I'm here."

He smiled and brushed a hand over her cheek.

"Good. Good." He glanced at Evan and the doctor. "You did as I asked?"

What was with all of this secrecy?

"Aye, George. I did," Doctor Dargavel said. "The cleric and solicitor should be here within the hour."

Cleric? Solicitor?

Sophronie stifled a wail of despair.

"I would like to know precisely what my father's condition is, Doctor."

He gave her a grave look, then sighed and nodded. "I feared when he was trampled that he'd suffered internal injuries. There's nae way to be absolutely positive, of course, and as he was recoverin' well, I concluded he had no'. Unfortunately, today when he took a tumble and struck his already bruised spleen, it ruptured."

Faintness swept Sophronie, and she struggled to keep her wits about her.

Even she knew what a ruptured spleen meant. Papa was bleeding to death. Right before her eyes, though she couldn't see the blood, her beloved father's life source was slowly ebbing away.

This is so unfair! she screamed inside her mind.

"I didn't tumble." Papa stared directly at Evan. "That woman pushed me with her horse after I told her it was none of her business when Sophronie and I were returning to Virginia."

Evan and Sophronie swung astounded glances to her father.

"Miss Wesleyan attacked you with her mount?"

"She did." He gave a weak nod.

"The vile bitch." Sophronie clenched her teeth against the litany of profanity threatening to spill forth.

Evan made a rough sound in his throat and tramped to the window to peer out.

"In any event, Miss Slater, yer father will no' recover," the doctor said.

Scalding tears slipped down her cheeks.

"Oh, Papa. How can I bear to go on without you?"

Utterly heartbroken, she laid her head upon his mattress.

He smoothed his hand over her hair. "I want you and the duke to wed, my dear. Tonight. As soon as the

149

cleric arrives. I'm writing a new will and leaving the Duke of Waycross half of my estate. He has already agreed to the union."

"What? *What?*" Sophronie shook her head, swinging her attention from her father to Evan and back to her father again. "No," she gasped. "You cannot be serious. It's absurd."

She couldn't breathe. Her heart was pounding so hard, it threatened to break through the walls of her chest. A roaring began in her ears and black dots flickered before her eyes. She clutched the edge of the mattress and forced air into her constricted lungs.

I shall not faint. I shall not.

Evan was nothing more than a scheming, manipulating opportunist.

Had he suggested this nefarious plan?

"I am absolutely serious, daughter. The duke will protect you and care for you. He understands your love of horses better than any other man I have met. He is a good match for you."

Fury sizzled in her blood toward Evan and betrayal toward her father. How could Papa put her in this wholly untenable position?

She jutted her chin out. "And if I refuse?"

Having grown impossibly paler yet, her father gazed at her for a lengthy, disquieting moment. "Then I shall have the solicitor put my estate in a trust for your children when they reach their majority, should you have any."

She gasped and recoiled as if he'd struck her.

"You...you would disinherit me?" Sophronie thought her heart couldn't break any further.

She'd been dead wrong.

"I am dying, Sophronie," Papa said gently. "I am doing what I believe in my heart is best for you. Many marriages are arranged, as you well know. Of all the men I know, the Duke of Waycross is my choice for you. I trust him. You are headstrong and obstinate. You flout convention and cock a snook at decorum, but I expect you to abide by my wishes in this. I can die peacefully knowing your future is secure and you are safe with an honorable man."

She'd argue that last point until her dying breath.

There was nothing honorable about Waycross

taking an heiress to wife for half of her father's fortune. There was a nasty term for that. Bribery. Nevertheless, it was her dying father's desperate if misguided attempt to keep his wayward daughter safe. Sophronie could hardly blame him for taking this desperate step.

All her life, she'd overstepped the mark and refused to toe the line. In this, her father's last request, she could honor him. Head bowed, she didn't try to stop the tears dripping from her eyes and splattering onto her hands and gown.

"Here, Sophronie." A starched white handkerchief appeared in her line of vision.

She inhaled a ragged breath and accepted the neat square. After blowing her nose and drying her face, she raised her head.

"Answer me one question, Papa, and swear upon my mother's and sister's and brother's grave that you will do so truthfully." She avoided looking in Evan's direction. Such rage thrummed through her at his deception that she wanted to pummel him. To punch him in the nose and draw blood.

"I have always been honest with you, Sophronie."

Her father gave her a sad, nascent smile. "You have been my sun and moon. You gave me a reason to keep living when I wanted to die after your mother and siblings died. Ask what you will, my dear."

"Whose idea was the union between the duke and me?" She crumpled the handkerchief into a ball and squeezed with all of her might, transferring her wrath, frustration, and grief to the innocent cloth. "Yours or his?"

She cut Evan a scorching, sidelong glance. This brute had caused her to doubt her beloved Papa for the first time in her life.

"It was all mine, my dear." Father flicked a glance to Evan. "He refuses to consider the union unless you willingly agree."

As if she had any real choice in the matter.

Filling her lungs with a shuddery breath, Sophronie pursed her lips. So be it, but she had contingencies of her own.

"I shall agree under specific conditions." She fisted her hand around the damp and hopelessly wrinkled handkerchief. "You both must agree to them in writing as well."

Sophronie would never forgive Evan for his part in this. Never. She didn't believe for one second he hadn't somehow coerced her father into this devious plan.

Her father's gaze grew shrewd and wary, but Evan's countenance remained inscrutable. He turned to face her and her father. His midnight-black hair stood on end as if he'd been scraping his fingers through the strands.

"Which are?" Papa asked cautiously, growing ever weaker before her eyes.

He knew his daughter well, and another time, his leeriness might've made her smile.

"If after a year the Duke of Waycross and I are irrevocably incompatible, I shall be allowed to leave and go where I choose without any reprisal from him. My half of your estate will remain in my control at all times."

"But what if there is a child?" Papa sent Evan a disturbed glance. "You cannot separate a child, especially if he is the heir, from his father."

Sophronie fixed Evan with a fulminating stare.

"The marriage will not be consummated until—if ever—I am convinced we are suitable. It would only be a year, and the duke can ask for an annulment."

Heat flared up her cheeks at having such an intimate discussion in front of her father and the doctor. Regardless, they'd conspired behind her back so they could squirm in discomfort too.

"I agree," Evan said in a tenor she'd never heard before, like something gathered from the deepest night. It sent a shiver from her waist to her spine and made her want to retract her verbal agreement.

"As do I." Her father managed a wan smile and patted her hand resting upon his mattress. "You are angry with me now, daughter, but in time, I think you will come to thank me."

A rustling in the passageway announced someone's arrival. After a soft knock on the doorframe, the duchess entered, accompanied by two gentlemen. "Mr. Cornett and Reverend Twitchell are here at yer behest, Mr. Slater. I thought it best to bring them up straightaway."

Her inquisitive gaze circled the men in the room before settling on Sophronie with sympathy.

"Mother, please ask the rest of the family to assemble here posthaste." Evan moved to stand behind Sophronie.

Already staking his claim, was he?

She looked momentarily nonplussed. "*All* of them?"

Over her shoulder, Sophronie glared daggers at him from beneath her spiky eyelashes. She bet he wanted to make sure there were plenty of witnesses to the marriage.

Unfair, her conscience promptly scolded. *You know how close Evan is to his family. He and they are being robbed of a proper wedding ceremony too.*

"Yes, Your Grace," Papa said to the duchess, his pale face wreathed in happiness. "Our children are to wed this very night."

11

Balston House—Duchess's Chambers
17 August 1810

As she had since Papa's funeral four days ago, Sophronie sat curled in the window seat in her new rooms. She'd thought the guest bedchamber lovely, but the duchess's suite was beyond exquisite. Swathed in shimmering gold, ivory, and various shades of greens and pinks, the entire décor shouted regal elegance. In addition to the bedchamber, the apartment included an enormous closet, a bathing room, a charming sitting room, and even a small chamber for a servant.

Her accommodations ought to hold her in thrall. However, grief cast a mantle of despondency over Sophronie, preventing her from enjoying or appreciating anything. Her heart ticked listlessly in her chest as she fingered the crisp black bombazine of her gown. She'd barely eaten and hadn't left her chamber since the funeral.

That didn't mean she'd been alone.

No, a constant stream of Evan's relatives checked on her several times a day. Each brought something to cheer her. A flower, a book, a feather, a sewing basket, confections from the kitchen, and her favorite of all, a dappled, long-haired black and white kitten with a black mustache and the most intense green eyes she'd ever seen, a gift from Grandmother Gordonstone.

"The wee laddie willna fill the ache in yer heart for yer father, my dear, but experience has taught me that havin' somethin' to love and that loves ye in return lessens the pain a wee bit." The kind elderly woman smelling of lavender and lilies had kissed Sophronie's cheek. "I am delighted ye are a part of the family. I kent from the moment I set eyes upon ye, it was meant to be."

Sophronie disagreed with that assessment but had refrained from saying so.

Sir Peppermint slept, curled into a tight ball, beside

her on the ivory padded window seat. Sophronie ran her fingers over his tiny head. He flicked his ears but slept on. How she wished she might sleep as soundly. Alas, slumber eluded her, for when she lay upon the great, soft mattress and closed her eyes, memories of her father paraded past her mind.

She missed him so much, her chest actually ached, and as it had for days, her throat burned with unshed tears.

Two days ago, she'd sent a letter to London requesting her possessions and Papa's be packed and shipped to Balston House. Another missive had been posted to Virginia for the same purpose. With the assistance of Evan's man of affairs, additional correspondences had been sent to Papa's solicitor in Virginia, his men of business in Virginia and London, various business associates, and the steward at their Virginia plantation.

There were other people Sophronie needed to write, but not now. Not when her grief was so new, she couldn't fathom how she would survive the pain.

She studied her hand where a wedding band ought

to rest—if she'd married for love. None did because she hadn't. Evan had made no mention of giving her one either. That only confirmed her suspicion that he was a fortune hunter and had seized an opportunity of a lifetime handed to him on a silver salver.

How very peculiar to think of herself as the Duchess of Waycross now. In truth, Sophronie couldn't as yet. Mayhap she never would, principally as she fully intended to leave once the obligatory year had passed. This interlude in Scotland was simply an unexpected detour on her journey in life.

Of her husband, she'd seen little. Faultlessly kind and considerate, he came to her bedchamber door every evening and wished her goodnight. That was the extent of their interactions. She had only begun to trust him, and this diabolical stunt—manipulating her father into giving Evan half of his wealth—proved she'd been right to be suspicious of him all along.

Of its own volition, her gaze meandered to the closed and locked door to his rooms visible through the open sitting-room door. That first night, she'd lain awake until dawn's muted colors peeked over the horizon listening for the harsh sound of the key scraping in the lock. It had never come, and after the third night, Sophronie realized Evan intended to keep his word.

Their marriage would not be consummated.

She was relieved beyond words and unrepentant in her ongoing qualms.

If anyone else in the household knew the peculiar relationship between the new Duchess of Waycross and the duke—and assuredly others must be aware—no one breathed a hint to Sophronie.

Leaning her head against the windowpane, she watched crystalline teardrop-shaped raindrop after raindrop trickle an irregular path down the glass. The rain had begun this morning and showed no sign of easing, although given it was August, assuredly it must.

Scotland's summer clime was much cooler than Virginia's sultry, humid heat. Regardless, Sophronie missed her childhood home, although she wasn't optimistic she'd return there when the year of her marriage to Evan came to an end.

Tilting her head as she petted Sir Peppermint, she searched the drive below.

Her luxuriant rooms overlooked the courtyard, and in the distance, past the keep, the corner of the stables was visible. She supposed that was deliberate, as the duchesses would've needed to know of the arrival and departure of their guests.

A soft scratching on the door preceded Larissa entering. Closest in age to Sophronie, Larissa had already formed a close, and what Sophronie hoped was a sisterly bond.

"I thought perhaps I could sit and read with ye or persuade ye to take refreshments with me in the library." Larissa waited at the entrance, always careful not to intrude.

Sophronie still hadn't explored the gallery that had so intrigued her. She would later, when her heart wasn't broken and she could breathe without fear of tears overcoming her.

Patting the tufted cushion beside her, she swung her legs to the floor to make room for Larissa.

"Please, sit with me, Larissa. I would enjoy your company on such a bleak day."

Grinning, her youngest sister-in-law closed the door and hurried to the window seat. "I asked the cook to make hot chocolate and shortbread for us."

Larissa plopped onto the seat, kicked her slippers off, and folded her legs beneath her before gathering Sir Peppermint into her arms. "Hello, precious." The kitten blinked sleepy bottle-green eyes at her and yawned widely. "I should've asked for warm milk for ye too."

"He ate not so long ago." Sophronie scratched his head as he began purring contentedly in Larissa's lap. "He's particularly fond of kippers."

"He can have mine then. I canna abide them or trout either." Larissa pulled a comical face. "Grandmother Larimore told me from the time I was a toddler that I'd learn to like them when I became an adult. She was wrong."

Evan's family had welcomed Sophronie into their depths with graciousness and warmth she hadn't expected. No one had questioned the hasty marriage nor made her feel unwanted.

A mud-spattered but obviously quality coach rumbled up the drive, and Larissa and Sophronie glanced out the rain-streaked window. Someone was either daring or extremely bored to venture out in this torrent.

"Are you expecting visitors today?" Sophronie asked her new sister-in-law.

Forehead scrunched, Larissa shook her head. "Nae." Her scowl deepened. "And certainly not *her*. Given the circumstances, she really should've sent a note 'round first."

A footman had run down the steps and held an umbrella over the woman's head, obstructing Sophronie's view. She squinted and angled her head to get a better view. "Who is it?"

"Leah Wesleyan." Larissa's unfriendly tone held no welcome.

Sophronie flashed cold, then hot, then cold again as rage sluiced through her. That woman dared to call here? After she'd sent Papa to an early grave?

Did she think she'd not suffer any consequences for what she did?

Good manners had required Evan to respond to Miss Wesleyan's parents' inquiry after Papa's health. After all, he'd collapsed at their house, and naturally, they were concerned. Evan told Sophronie he'd briefly explained that George Slater had quietly passed from this world in his sleep in the early morning hours.

Nevertheless, that viper had no right to intrude upon this household.

In an instant, Sophronie was on her feet and brushing the wrinkles from her gown. Forming a glacial smile, she yanked the bell pull and said over her shoulder, "Would you and the rest of the family care to join me in the drawing room when I receive her as the new duchess?"

"Och, aye!" Larissa set Sir Peppermint down and leaped to her feet, a mischievous grin splitting her pretty face. "I wouldna miss it for the world, and I'm sure they wouldna either."

A moment later, Coira, one of the maids, entered. "Ye rang for me, Yer Grace?"

No matter how often Sophronie told the servants not to address her with the honorific, they continued to do so.

"Please ask Blige to show our guest to the drawing room and ask Cook for tea and dainties. I shall be down shortly." As Sophronie turned toward her dressing table, she paused. "Please make sure no one mentions the duke's and my marriage."

Eyes huge and brimming with curiosity, Coira

bobbed a curtsy. "As ye wish, Yer Grace."

"I'll go tell the others, Roni." Larissa pressed a swift kiss to her cheek. "Ye needn't fret. We'll stand with ye. Ye are family now."

With that, she rushed from the room, no doubt eager to tell her relatives of the brewing storm.

Sophronie took several minutes to tidy her hair, pinch her cheeks to add a bit of color, and don a pair of black jet and diamond earrings. She might be in mourning, but she needn't look frumpy. After kissing Sir Peppermint on his soft forehead, she said, "I'm off to face the dragon, my sweet friend."

He batted at her earring, and Sophronie laughed. That she could amid such gut-wrenching sorrow astounded and encouraged her. Life would go on. She would go on and eventually know joy again. Somehow, even thinking such thoughts so early after Papa's death seemed traitorous.

"I have to leave you for a bit, darling. There's an evil witch below who needs putting in her place."

The lowest bowels of hell would serve nicely.

12

Balston House Drawing Room
Five minutes later

Not quite certain what to expect, Sophronie entered the drawing room to find the rest of the family assembled, including Evan. Except for his crisp neckcloth and shirt, he wore all black in honor of her father's passing. His severe togs gave him a debonair, dashing, and altogether too handsome appearance.

She had to remind herself he was a dishonest libertine. An opportunist whose machinations had landed him a fortune and a reluctant bride.

He flashed a rakish smile and made directly for her. Her stupid, traitorous heart flip-flopped, and her silly knees went wobbly as warm pudding. Self-disgust pummeled her. How could she still find him attractive when he'd revealed his true character?

Was that a twinkle in his eye?

She'd almost forgotten—*almost*—that she'd ever believed him glum and taciturn.

Miss Wesleyan, resplendent in a white gown with a holly-berry red ribbon at her trim waist and roses of the same shade embroidered into an overskirt, didn't bother turning her head upon Sophronie's entrance. Her white bonnet and spencer, trimmed with the same cheerful shade of red braid, accented her dark hair and pale skin to perfection.

Sophronie would vow the woman had purposefully worn white because she knew Sophronie would be in mourning black and wanted to magnify the difference between the women.

That Miss Wesleyan had the nerve to come to Balston House after what she had done to Papa rubbed Sophronie raw. She'd wished for charges to be brought against Miss Wesleyan, but it would've been the heiress's word against Papa's. With him dead and with no witnesses, there was no one to corroborate his story.

The question of why he'd been on that side of the house in the first place might never be answered. It haunted Sophronie, but there was nothing she could do about it.

"Thank you, Evan." She accepted Evan's extended arm and gave a satisfied inner smile when Miss Wesleyan's finely plucked eyebrows drew together at Sophronie's use of his given name.

"Sit here, Sophronie." Larissa scooted farther to the side, leaving an opening between her and Sarah. Rosalind sat on Sarah's other side, and their four aunts had wandered to stand behind the burgundy and gold brocade settee. Like protective sentinels, her new aunts stood guard, each ready to defend her should the need arise.

Emotion welled in Sophronie's chest at their show of solidarity for her.

Evan guided her to the vacant seat then went to stand before the intricately carved walnut mantel. A cozy fire snapped and crackled in the hearth, shooting orange, blue, and crimson flames toward the chimney behind the brass scrolled screen.

Perhaps this afternoon she'd spend a few quiet hours in the gallery. It was a perfect day for reading.

Hands behind his back, Evan faced the room. His grandmothers and mother sat upon the other settee while Miss Wesleyan had claimed an armchair at one end of the rosewood tea table, much like a queen upon her throne, overseeing her minions.

"It is so good of you to join us, Miss Slater." The smile Miss Wesleyan fashioned didn't quite reach her blue eyes.

Who did she think she was, acting like *she* was the hostess?

"I didn't expect you to inconvenience yourself. I simply came to offer my sincerest condolences at the loss of your father. How unfortunate that he didn't regain consciousness before passing so that you might've said farewell."

Sophronie sent Evan a private look.

The silence became so deafening, a pin might've dropped in the room and reverberated like a cannon's explosion. Not one of Evan's relatives disputed Miss Wesleyan though each knew her to be inaccurate.

That was curious. Had Evan cautioned them against saying anything?

Why?

"Trust him," Larissa whispered as she slid her hand into Sophronie's, and Sophronie gave her a grateful look.

"It's no inconvenience, Miss Wesleyan." Slipping her hand from Larissa's, Sophronie accepted the steaming cup of tea Anna, now the dowager duchess, offered her. "Papa's loss will be strongly felt by many for a good while."

Aware Evan's blue-gray gaze rested upon her, Sophronie took a sip and damned her nerves to the lowest level of hell. She wished Miss Leah Wesleyan a speedy journey to Hades too, accompanied by a horde of tormenting demons.

Miss Wesleyan gave Evan a coquettish look from beneath her lashes, but he didn't return her flirtatious smile. A flicker of uncertainty glinted in her eyes for an instant before vanishing behind her perfected mask of feminine confidence.

"I'm sure you are anticipating returning to your

home in America," she said with as much sincerity as a thief apologizing to his robbery victim. "It does so help to be surrounded by familiar and comfortable environs when one is grieving the loss of a loved one."

"Ye would ken this because ye have experienced such a loss yerself?" Aunt Christina asked, clearly not believing a word of Miss Wesleyan's insincere diatribe.

Aunt Katryne said, "We have, ye ken. Our father and brother, and several of us have lost husbands too."

Miss Wesleyan squirmed on her seat, much like the proverbial canary cornered by a hungry cat. "Not I personally, per se. But I am acquainted with several people who have suffered a tragic loss."

"No' the same thing at all," Grandmother Gordonstone said with a stern look. "If a horse steps on my foot, ye willna feel the pain."

"Ah, yes. I see your point." Miss Wesleyan pasted a bright smile on her face and looked expectantly at Sophronie. "Do you sail soon?"

Sophronie would give her credit for persistence. Rather like a rat after of morsel of bread.

She selected a ginger biscuit and took a bite. She'd

draw this torment out as long as she could. Miss Leah Wesleyan had thought to become the next Duchess of Waycross, but her devious actions had cost her that coveted position. They'd also cost Sophronie her freedom and her beloved father, and she would enjoy every second of the woman's discomfort.

"Whyever would I do that, Miss Wesleyan?" Sophronie asked nonchalantly as she sent Evan a radiant smile, hoping he'd comprehend the game she played.

He gallantly responded with a roguish smile and a devilish wink for good measure.

Let Miss Wesleyan stew on that for a bit.

Rosalind snorted, and Sarah giggled behind her hand.

Blinking rather idiotically, Miss Wesleyan looked from person to person.

Evan rubbed his nose, and Sophronie swore his lips twitched.

Warmth infused her.

Yes, he knew exactly what she was about.

"Well, because… Surely you want to go home at the earliest opportunity," Miss Wesleyan prodded, clumsily crossing from politesse into indiscretion. She was in such a rush to see Sophronie gone from Scotland that she was practically pushing her out the door. A wonder she didn't offer to pack Sophronie's trunks, book her passage, and personally escort her to the docks.

Sophronie set her ginger biscuit down and patted her mouth with a serviette.

"But Balston House *is* my home, Miss Wesleyan."

Sophronie cast a smile around the room, taking in her new family. Each beamed back at her, and her heart lifted a trifle. These were good people. People she'd like to get to know better and enjoy a relationship with.

Evan might've stepped in at any moment and spared Miss Wesleyan her vexation, but apparently, he'd decided to permit Sophronie this triumph. She forgave him a smidge for his part in the plot to save her from unidentified villains in her future by making her his duchess.

She was perfectly capable of looking after herself, thank you very much.

Miss Wesleyan's winged eyebrows nearly touched as they swooped together in her bewilderment. She focused on Evan's mother. Leaning forward, she fashioned an affable smile designed to elicit trust. "Please forgive me, but I am somewhat confused, Duchess—"

"Oh, it's dowager duchess now, Miss Wesleyan." Eyes alight with mirth, Evan's mother observed her guest over the rim of her teacup.

Sophronie adored her new mother-in-law at that moment.

"What?" Miss Wesleyan blurted. Utterly flummoxed, she furrowed her forehead in consternation. "I beg your pardon? I misheard you, I'm certain."

"We are *all* simply delighted." Grandmother Larimore hollered before grinning from ear to ear. "Brilliant choice. Positively brilliant."

"What is brilliant?" Miss Wesleyan asked, searching the older woman's wrinkled features.

One of the aunts muttered beneath her breath, "That one has always been a brainless beauty."

"Thick as an oak stump," another agreed.

"Would someone please explain to me why Miss Slater says Balston House is her home?" Miss Wesleyan asked shrilly, with a thunderous glower toward Evan's aunts having a bit of fun at her expense.

"Oh, for pity's sake. Enough of this intelligence-robbing twaddle." Rosalind threw her hands into the air, and with a shake of her head, speared Miss Wesleyan with an unsympathetic look. "Sophronie and Evan are married. *She* is the Duchess of Waycross now."

13

Still in the Drawing Room

A good dozen tick-tocks of the mantel clock later

Evan suspected what Sophronie had planned when the maid said the new duchess didn't want anyone discussing the marriage before she arrived in the drawing room. He'd permitted his wife her revenge. God knew she'd deserved it after what Leah had done.

Without raising her voice or revealing her ire, his new wife had taken Leah down several well-deserved pegs.

"If everyone would excuse us, my wife and I would like a few moments with Miss Wesleyan."

Alarm crinkled Leah's features before she smoothed them into artificial composure once more.

She was caught, and she well knew it.

"Of course, my dear." Mother stood and helped her mother to her feet. "Let's allow them a few moments' privacy, shall we?"

Sarah kissed Sophronie's cheek then said without making any attempt to lower her voice, "Give her hell. For all of us. It's nae more than she deserves."

Sophronie and Leah remained seated as the women filed from the room, and Rosalind, after a final murderous glare at Leah's back, closed the door.

Evan took a seat beside his wife and placed his hand upon hers atop her thigh.

She stiffened slightly but didn't object or withdraw her hand.

"You are truly wed? The vows were spoken before a cleric?" Leah asked stiffly, making no attempt to hide her dislike of Sophronie.

"We are, indisputably," Evan said. "I've sworn to protect Sophronie for the rest of our lives, and that is why I'm grateful ye called today. If ye had no', I intended to pay ye a visit in a day or two."

"Why?" Leah asked bitterly, making no attempt to

hide her profound disappointment.

Beside him, he felt Sophronie quivering with suppressed rage. He had no doubt she'd never struggled so hard to hold her tongue and perhaps refrain from ripping Leah's hair from her intricately styled coiffeur.

"We ken what ye did at Kirnochshire Manor the day of the fair," Evan said, studying Leah for signs of guilt.

He wasn't disappointed.

Nostrils flaring, Leah went perfectly still and looked to the side away from them. "I have no idea what you are implying, but I take exception to your tone and insinuation."

"Allow me to elucidate for you." Sophronie set aside her teacup, her composure on par with Almack's peeresses. "My father was *perfectly* lucid for several hours before he died. He told us *you* attacked him with your horse when he declined to inform you when we were sailing for America."

Sophronie held Leah's stare, refusing to cow under the other woman's snooty demeanor.

Evan wanted to applaud her courage.

"Bah! Utter rubbish," Leah said, hatred and fury dripping from each clipped syllable. "You can prove nothing."

"Dinna be so sure," Evan said. "The physician confirmed the cause of injury, and ye were seen."

"*What*? When? By whom?" Sophronie yanked her hand free and jerked her head in his direction. "Why didn't you tell *me*?"

Her pleading tone cleaved his heart wide open.

Evan peered into her tumultuous eyes, willing her to stay calm and listen. "I had to complete the investigation first. To have irrefutable evidence before I made such a serious accusation."

"I don't believe you," Leah said, rising. "And I shan't stay and be further insulted."

"Ye will leave when I say ye can. Sit down," Evan ordered, pointing to the chair. "Now."

She would hear him out because Sophronie deserved to know the truth.

Visibly shaken, her face leached of all color, Leah sank back onto the chair.

"Yer first mistake was to order a servant to ask

George Slater to meet ye. A servant ye've no' treated well. Why Slater agreed, I cannot imagine."

"I revealed that I had information about his daughter that would cause a scandal." She smirked. "It was a lie, of course, but your smudged reputation preceded you, Miss Slater. Your father was eager to learn what mischief you'd embroiled yourself in this time and to protect you from the consequence."

A small gasp escaped Sophronie.

As if she hadn't revealed herself as a lying, conniving wench, Leah fingered her spencer's top clasp. "His devotion was really quite touching."

"She is the Duchess of Waycross to ye, and ye would do well to address my wife with the respect and honor a woman of her station deserves," Evan snapped.

Sophronie's eyes grew wide and then softened slightly at his defense of her. He knew she believed he'd manipulated her father into agreeing to an arranged marriage between them and even now schemed to steal half of her fortune from her.

That he hadn't done any such thing made no difference if she believed otherwise. In time, he hoped to convince her. She'd been halfway to winning his heart, and Evan had hoped she would soften toward him. Now a chasm had sprouted up between them so vast and so deep, he didn't know how to breach the gap.

Eyes flashing with fury, Leah pursed her lips together as if she could barely restrain the retort kicking at the back of her teeth.

"Secondly, ye assumed yer guests were on the greens. However, Mrs. Honeyforth developed a migraine, and her daughter accompanied her to her chamber." Evan angled his head as he watched understanding dawn on Leah's face. "Their rooms faced the east side of the house, and Miss Honeyforth happened to glance out the window when she heard voices. She called her mother over, and they witnessed ye rammin' yer horse into George Slater."

Leah wilted like a rose tossed onto burning coals.

"How could you?" Sophronie's eyes misting with anger and grief. "My father was a gentle soul, a kind, decent, and honorable man, and you killed him. Why?"

"I wanted to get rid of *you*," Leah snarled. "I've waited years to become the Duchess of Waycross, and I wasn't about to let you—*an upstart American*—usurp what was mine."

Hatred rendered her voice strident and brittle and lifted the pitch to the ceiling.

"Ye were never goin' to become my duchess," Evan said in even tones despite the anger heating his blood. "Ye were unsuitable in every way that truly counted."

She gasped and flinched, closing her eyes for a moment.

No guilt or pity chastised him for his directness.

"I have written confessions from yer servant—who, by the way, is now in my employ— as well as the ladies' sworn testimonies." Evan slid an arm around Sophronie, who trembled like a leaf in a gale. That she'd remained silent was a blessed miracle.

"What do you want of me?" Miss Wesleyan asked, shoulders slumping in defeat. She was careful to direct her question to Evan and to avoid looking in Sophronie's direction.

Likely, Sophronie would've told her exactly what she'd like her to do in the most indelicate of terms, except Evan held one of her hands and gave it a preemptive warning squeeze.

"Ye will leave Scotland, and ye will no' return as long as I, my wife, or our children draw breath. If ye do, I shall turn those incriminatin' letters over to the magistrate without a second thought."

Sophronie leaned into his side, seeming to need his strength. Tremors shook her slight frame, though from anger or shock, he couldn't discern.

He kissed her forehead as if he'd done so many times before.

"Do ye understand, Leah?" Evan didn't feel a morsel of pity for her. If it wouldn't mean dragging Sophronie's reputation through the mud, he'd have Leah arrested today. Also, Evan wasn't convinced a jury would convict her as George Slater had already been gravely injured.

"I understand," she said sourly, eviscerating him and Sophronie with an acrimonious glare.

"Ye have four and twenty hours to pack and depart." Evan wasn't giving her an opportunity to retaliate against his wife or family. "I dinna care what excuse ye give yer family. Just ensure ye heed me."

She stood, haughty and superior even in her disgrace. "Choosing that American bumpkin over me makes you a laughing stock, Evan. You're a fool, and soon everyone will know what a monumental mistake you've made marrying so far beneath you."

He grinned. "A happy fool. You'd have made me and my family miserable. They adore Sophronie, as do I."

With a final hate-filled glower toward Sophronie, Leah stormed from the drawing room.

He met Sophronie's bemused eyes and arched eyebrows. "Adore me, do you?"

"Aye, more than ye can ken."

Lifting her chin, he searched her eyes then captured her mouth in a searing kiss. He'd longed to kiss her again ever since that day when they'd been riding. She relaxed in his arms and twined her arms about his neck.

At his gentle prodding, she opened her mouth to him, and Evan swept his tongue inside the sweet cavern. She tasted of ginger and tea, and her subtle fragrance—lilacs and lilies—wrapped around him, magnifying the heady sensations thrumming through him.

"Sophronie," he groaned, pulling away. "I want to ken ye as a real husband, but I willna until ye are willin'."

She drew away, confusion shining in her eyes. Shaking her head, she stood. "I cannot. We'd be tied together for the rest of our lives if I do as you bid."

"Would that be so bad, lass?" He reached his hand out and brushed a knuckle over her silken cheek.

"Not for you," she snapped. "You have what you were after. I, on the other hand, have been denied my choice of a husband."

"Nae matter what ye believe, until yer father approached me, I'd never considered a match between us." That wasn't entirely true. After their kiss, he'd given the notion a full sixty seconds of contemplation before discarding it as insane. Why would he marry a woman who vexed the hell out of him most of the time?

He refrained from saying that to the spitfire sitting beside him, however.

She spread her hands apart, heartache and betrayal awash in her azure eyes. "Don't you understand, Evan?

No matter how long we are married, I shall always believe I was merely the means to an end. As a person, I had no value except what I brought to the union—my father's fortune."

Tired of being made to feel the villain when his primary intention had been to protect her at great detriment to his personal wishes, Evan made a harsh sound in his throat.

"If I'd wanted to wed an heiress, I needn't have waited for ye, Sophronie. Leah Wesleyan has been willin' for several years." Anger at himself and Sophronie sizzled through his blood. He'd sacrificed his chance at marrying for love too, but she conveniently placed all of the blame at his feet.

"What's more, Leah is Scots and as refined a lady as can be found in England. We were far more well-matched than ye and I. Regardless, I chose to honor the wishes of a dyin' man whom I admired and respected because his greatest concern was for yer future."

Lips parted, Sophronie stared at him, her eyes alarmingly blue in her ashen face. She slowly rose, her movements as precise and stiff as a woman five decades older.

"You do realize, Evan, that you've just confirmed that you find me inferior in every way to a scheming, devious murderess."

Hell's bells.

He had, and that hadn't been his intent at all.

She closed her eyes, the sweep of her lashes dark against her pale cheeks. She opened her eyes, resignation and pain shining in their depths, and Evan would've done anything to erase the anguish from her features.

"This marriage was a colossal mistake." Her lower lip quavered, but she summoned control. "For both of our sakes, I shall not wait a year to have it annulled."

Shite.

She sucked in a ragged breath, her voice a mere thread of sound. "I want to return to Virginia. I want to see my horse, who I miss almost as much as Papa. I want my old life back with all of its imperfections and flaws, Evan." A single crystalline droplet made a path down her cheek. "Most of all, I don't want to be a duchess."

She presented her back and swept toward the

entrance.

"Sophronie, wait." Christ, he shouldn't have lost his temper. "Ye cannot request an annulment yet. Yer father's will is very clear. Ye willna have access to yer portion of his estate should the marriage end before the one-year term."

She half-turned, her features ravaged with hurt and remorse. "Unlike you, Evan, I would rather give up a fortune than be trapped in a loveless marriage. I'm returning to Virginia at the first opportunity."

"I willna permit it." When she calmed down, she'd see reason. Sophronie was a sensible woman.

"How do you plan on stopping me? Make me a prisoner?" With that, she swept from the room.

Nae, not a prisoner, but he could make it impossible for her to leave. She'd underestimated a husband's influence and power. She might be ready to give up on their marriage after less than a week, but Evan was not.

14

Balston House Gardens

9 September 1810

Sophronie fingered a yellow rose petal as Sir Peppermint frolicked among the flowers and bushes. Papa had been gone for a month. How could the time have gone by so swiftly? What was more, Sophronie was no closer to having her marriage annulled than she had been four weeks ago.

The day was pleasantly warm with a slight breeze. However, she smelled autumn in the air, and she'd heard chatter amongst the servants that it might be a harsh winter. That necessitated her leaving sooner rather than later.

A rook called to its mate as it flew overhead.

Sophronie followed the bird's graceful flight to the Scotch pine forest bordering the meadow behind the castle. Perhaps she'd take a ride or a walk over there today. There was much of the keep's grounds she'd yet to explore.

Her possessions had arrived from London along with letters of condolences from several of her friends. Each had invited her to visit whenever and for as long as she'd liked. She hadn't shared her farce of a marriage, but Leah Wesleyan had, the miserable wretch.

Lifting the letter she'd just read from Jessica Rolston, Duchess of Bainbridge, to scan the neat script once more, Sophronie pressed her lips together and heaved a frustrated sigh. Miss Wesleyan had heeded Evan's threat and departed Scotland. She'd made straight for London and used her wealth and beauty to pry open a few Society doors.

I am so sorry to hear of your father's passing. Please accept my heartfelt condolences. It seems I should offer you felicitations as well. I understand you are now the Duchess of Waycross.

I confess that news imparted by Miss Leah Wesleyan came as a great surprise. I quite thought you couldn't abide the duke. I wish you every happiness, dear friend. I do hope that means I shall see more of you in the future as I cannot think you will return to Virginia.

Speaking of Miss Wesleyan, she is a most trying individual. She puts on such airs, and never have I encountered a woman more determined to marry a title. She has little enough kind to say about you and your marriage to the duke. Rest assured, your friends in London have risen to your defense, and many doors have been closed to her already.

Sir Peppermint charged from his hiding place in a bush and attacked the hem of Sophronie's skirt. "What are you about, young rascal?" She squatted and tickled his stomach. He tolerated her ministrations for a few seconds, then twisted away and dashed off again.

Smiling at his antics, Sophronie folded the letter and slipped it into her pocket. "I'm not surprised that witch is gossiping about my marriage."

"Who is?"

Sophronie wheeled around, her heart thundering in her chest. "Evan, you startled me."

"I apologize, lass. I dinna mean to."

Hatless, as was his wont, his boots and trousers were covered with specks of dust and dirt. Likely he'd been training horses again today. Even so unkempt, he was more striking than any man of her acquaintance. Just a few short weeks ago, she'd thought him rough and uncouth. Now she found his rugged good looks devastatingly appealing.

She'd love to have been invited to partake in the breeding and training. However, other than permitting her to ride horseback, Evan hadn't included her in anything regarding his horses.

"It's of no import." Her bonnet blocked most of the afternoon sun from her eyes, but as he was so much taller than her, she had to look upward. Shielding her eyes from the glare with her hand, she said, "How is the training going?"

"Fair enough." He cupped his nape and gave her a sidelong look. "Ye are welcome to visit the broodmare ye purchased at Tattersalls's. I ken ye were taken with her."

Lowering her hand, Sophronie started to shake her head then stopped. "Perhaps I shall."

A boyish grin kicked up on one side of his mouth as if her answer pleased him greatly. "Who's been gossipin' about our marriage?"

Who wasn't?

Word of the rushed nuptials had spread fast. Naturally, no one dared say anything directly to Sophronie's face, but she'd suffered many an inquisitive glance and ignored many more whispers behind hands.

"It matters not." Sophronie perused the garden for a sign of her playful kitten. He pounced on a round rock and batted it with his paw. Marshaling her courage, she scratched her nose.

"I should like to speak with a solicitor about the annulment, Evan." At once, his features turned to granite, but she pressed onward. "As you know, it's been a month since we exchanged vows. The more time passes, the more difficult it will be to get one granted."

"Nae." Giving a single shake of his head, causing a raven lock to fall over his forehead, he placed his hands upon her shoulders. In profoundly gentle tones, he said, "Roni, I am yer husband, like it or no', and I am responsible for yer wellbein'. I willna allow ye to do somethin' impulsive and rash that ye will later regret, lass."

"Why are you being so stubborn about this?" Pulling away from him, she fought back tears of anger and frustration. "You have your fortune. What else do you want?"

He was silent for several achingly long heartbeats, and she waited tensely, hoping for what she knew not.

At last, he filled his lungs with air, his chest expanding, and heaved a sigh. "I am a man of honor, and I swore a vow to yer father. One year."

He caught the violet ribbon fluttering against her chin and gave it a little tug.

"Don't you want to choose your wife because you care for her, Evan, instead of having settled on me?" Yes, marriages were arranged for convenience all of the time. Nonetheless, neither she nor Evan was the type to be content in such a match or to accept mediocrity in anything they undertook.

"I'm no' unhappy with ye, Roni. In truth, I think we could be verra happy together." Grinning, he tugged her closer. He smelled of horses. Other women might've been put off by the earthliness of his aroma, but she found it intoxicating. "I seem to recall yer father sayin' we had much in common."

Feeling oddly hollow, she gave him a sad smile. "I had begun to think so, but now I don't even know my own mind anymore."

He pointed his attention to his boots for a moment and toed the gravel. He raised turbulent blue-gray eyes to hers. "I hope ye'll decide to stay, because I wish it above all else. But if after a year, yer heart is set on leavin', I will let ye go. Be sure that is what ye want, because there are some things a person canna turn back from."

With that, he pivoted on his heels and strode away. Capturing her lower lip between her teeth, Sophronie watched her husband's long-legged stride take him farther and farther from her.

Is it what I want?

A month ago, filled with anger and grief and an overwhelming sense of betrayal, Sophronie had been positive an annulment was the answer. Now, she wasn't altogether sure.

15

Balston House Stables
One week later—early morning

Evan felt Sophronie's presence before he saw her.
It was as if his soul was in tune with hers and
sensed when she was near. His spirit cried out for hers,
and in her presence, he was at peace. If only she felt the
same, but given she'd asked again for an annulment last
week, his confidence to woo her was waning.

Bent at the waist and forearms resting on the top
railing, he'd been watching the two-, three-, and four-
year-olds romping in their pasture. These majestic
creatures were his future and that of the duchy's too. He
hadn't spent a cent of the money George Slater had left
him. It remained in a bank in Glasgow, earning interest.

There'd been no need, as the earnings from the investments he'd inherited and which were paid out quarterly were more than sufficient to meet his needs. Always frugal, he had no intention of changing his ways simply because he'd come into unexpected wealth.

The money from Slater would go to the man's grandchildren—if Evan and Sophronie had children. With a fervency and a desire that caused his lungs to cramp, Evan prayed it would be so someday.

"Good mornin'," he stated simply as she moved to his side. She wore her boy's garments today. His only objection to her garb was the decadent view the trousers provided of the swell of her hips and the plump pillows of her heart-shaped bottom. He'd have to punch any man senseless who looked his pleasure.

Evan notched his chin in the horses' direction. "They're feelin' frisky this morn."

"I can see that," she said with a hint of humor in her voice. "They are such magnificent creatures, aren't they, especially when they are running free? Graceful, spirited, powerful, and majestic."

"When I bestride him, I soar, I am a hawk. He trots

the air, the earth sings when he touches it."

At Sophronie's incredulous look, Evan gave her a sheepish grin. "Shakespeare."

Eyes shining, she gave him a slow smile. One of comradery, as if they shared an intimate secret that only the two of them knew.

"The air of heaven is that which blows between a horse's ears." She stepped onto the lowest rail and still was several inches shorter than Evan. "That's an Arabian proverb."

"What was yer first horse's name?" Evan didn't know why he asked, but he didn't want this new unspoken unity between them to end.

Her face took on a faraway look, and a secret smile arced her pink lips. "Sammy. He was a white pony. A gift for my fifth birthday. I had been riding for two years by then."

"Sammy? No' Sugar or Snowflake or Cotton?"

She made a face at him then climbed up to perch on the top rail. "That was his name when Papa bought him. I didn't think it was fair to make him learn another." Hands at her sides to balance her bottom, Sophronie cut him a sidelong look. "What about you? What was your first horse's name?"

Evan chuckled and climbed up to sit beside her. Only a couple of inches separated their thighs. He hadn't done this in decades. Not since he was a young lad. Even then, he'd been fascinated with horseflesh. "He was a geldin' named Sandy. I was eight years old."

"So I've been riding longer than you have," she said with such glee, he couldn't help but chuckle.

"Ye're a wee competitive thing, aren't ye?" He nudged her shoulder with his.

She shrugged. "I suppose I am."

They sat in companionable silence for several minutes, each lost in their own thoughts. The sun rose above the Scotch pine forest in the distance. "We probably should return to the house for breakfast."

With a nod, Sophronie swung a leg over the rail then jumped to the ground. She glanced at the horses. "This was nice. Thank you for letting me intrude."

"Ye're never an intrusion, lass." He took her hand and began to lead her toward the manor house. "I enjoy yer company."

After several paces, she withdrew her hand from his. She searched his face, her expression a mixture of bewilderment and wariness. "I need to change before breaking my fast. I'll see you then."

She broke into a trot.

She was running away. Evan was convinced she felt this thing blooming between them, but Sophronie, being Sophronie, fought her feelings every step of the way.

"Ye canna run forever, my obstinate lass. I mean to chase ye until ye run into my arms."

16

Balston House Library Gallery
12 October 1810

Sophronie glanced up from the book she'd been reading as Larissa climbed the narrow staircase to the gallery. The small balcony had become a favored place for reading, thinking, and occasionally napping.

Her sister-in-law looked especially pretty in one of her new morning gowns, a fern green and burgundy frock that flattered her coloring. She'd woven a burgundy ribbon through her curls and looked as fetching as Sophronie had ever seen her.

That might be on account of their new neighbors' very eligible and very handsome son who had called to introduce himself three weeks ago and who'd visited several times since.

"I thought I might find ye here," Larissa said, perching on the arm of Sophronie's chair. "What are ye readin'?"

Smiling, Sophronie tapped a page of the open book in her lap. "*Castle Rackrent.* I am taking a break from animal husbandry books."

"I should think so." Larissa scrunched her nose. "I mean, the act is quite basic. Evan doesna think we ken anythin' about his horse breedin', but we're no' blind."

Sir Peppermint, curled on the nearby couch, opened an eye. Evidently deciding nothing of import was happening, he closed his eye and resumed his nap.

"You look exceptionally lovely this morning, Larissa."

Larissa blushed and smoothed her hands down the front of the gown. "I only finished it yesterday."

"Well, it's most becoming." Sophronie made a mental note of the page then closed her novel. "I confess, I envy you your talent. I'm sorely lacking when it comes to sewing."

That was the case for most feminine pursuits, truth

to tell.

"We missed ye at breakfast this mornin', Roni." Larissa would bite her tongue off before prying, but everyone knew things were strained between Sophronie and Evan.

"I had a tray in my chamber quite early, then took a brisk walk to see the foals," Sophronie said. She'd done so often these past weeks and frequently took dinner in her chamber too. Her feelings for Evan had taken an unexpected turn, and if she spent too much time with him, she feared she'd never want to leave.

Then where would she be?

A woman hopelessly in love with the man who'd only married her for her money.

Larissa merely nodded and didn't pry.

Homesickness like none Sophronie had ever known while Papa was alive assailed her, and many were the nights she, who disdained weepy females, cried herself to sleep. She missed Cinnamon more and more each day. If she'd had any inkling that she'd be away from Virginia for so long, she'd have brought the mare with her. As it was, she didn't know when she'd next see her beloved horse.

Rather than behave like a man whose wife was intent on leaving him, Evan was wooing her, she'd vow. He'd even asked her opinion regarding several horse breeding and estate matters.

Not that she would permit herself to be lulled into the snare Evan was setting. She'd trusted him once. To do so again made her a numbskull. Never mind that her fickle heart thumped irregularly each time she saw him and that he grew impossibly more handsome too.

She found herself listening for his distinctive footfall or his melodic brogue.

When he smiled at her, half the time every thought in her head flew away while a warm sensation like sweet, rich hot chocolate infused every pore.

Evan was frustratingly polite and irritatingly kind but utterly uncompromising. She recalled when she'd broached the annulment last month. "I am yer husband, like it or no', and I am responsible for yer wellbein'. I willna allow ye to do somethin' impulsive and rash that ye will later regret, lass."

She'd already done that when she agreed to Papa's

dying wish and married the Scottish scoundrel, now her husband. Bringing her thoughts back to the present, she touched the fabric of Larissa's gown.

"Are you expecting company today?"

Her cheeks turning pink, Larissa nodded. "We're havin' guests for luncheon."

If Sophronie had taken on her duties as duchess as she would've done if she'd intended to remain, she'd have known guests were expected. Part of her rebellion against Evan's dictates was to refuse to assume the role and responsibilities of his duchess. Yes, it was petty, but there was no need to act like Evan's wife when she fully intended to pursue an annulment.

Didn't she?

Of course she did.

Then why hadn't she broached the subject in weeks now?

Evan seemed to know exactly what she was about and humored her. Not once had he reprimanded her on her dereliction of duty or suggested she ought to do more to help. Which, perversely, irritated her all the more.

Why, she was on the verge of becoming a veritable shrew.

Naturally, Anna was confused and curious about Sophronie's reluctance, but she hadn't pressed the issue.

"When ye are ready, dear, ye've only to tell me. I ken it is a lot to take in, marryin' so suddenly. Ye're still grievin' too."

Sophronie was, but her frustration toward Evan helped to buffer the pain of her father's passing.

As much as she wanted to paint Evan the ogre, he was proving himself otherwise. He'd permitted his womenfolk a few new gowns and other essentials, but to Sophronie's surprise, had limited their purchases. Not one of his female relatives had complained about his budget constraints.

He certainly could afford to buy entirely new wardrobes for all of them now, from their undergarments to pelisses and wraps and fallalls and fripperies. His frugalness was admirable, and it also chafed at Sophronie's conscience. His decency made her feel as if she were being unfair to him.

Unfair to him? She scoffed inwardly. Hardly.

He was the one who'd benefited from their union. Not her. Neither of them could deny that judicious slice of truth.

Why would a man who'd acquired a fortune be such a pinch-penny?

It made no sense.

Larissa pulled a small cloth-covered box wrapped in a bright yellow ribbon from her pocket. "Joyous birthday to ye, Sophronie."

Sophronie exhaled as she looked at the gift.

"How did you know?" she whispered, touched at Larissa's kindness.

"Evan told us."

"Oh." The marriage certificate had included their dates of birth. He'd noticed hers, but she hadn't his. That knowledge made her feel petulant and selfish.

"When is his birthday?"

Larissa gave her an odd look. "Next month. The twenty-first."

"I shall have to make a note of it."

"We always have a grand dinner party." Larissa giggled and rolled her eyes. "Evan's quite fond of his birthday celebration. He always makes certain our birthdays are memorable too."

"How thoughtful of him." Sophronie didn't trust herself to say more and chance ruining Larissa's kind gesture. She unwrapped the box then removed the lid. Inside lay a needlepoint bookmark with a kitten's face, strongly resembling Sir Peppermint.

"Oh, Larissa." Emotion clogged her throat.

"It's supposed to be Sir Peppermint, but I couldn't quite get his cheeks right."

"It's a wonderful likeness." Sophronie touched the kitten with her forefinger. "Thank you." She hugged her sister-in-law. "I always wanted sisters. I'm so glad I have them now."

Mayhap not for much longer. The thought brought a stab of pain to her heart.

If only Evan had loved her, then she'd have better understood the deal he made with Papa. She wouldn't have liked it, but she'd not live with perpetual doubt about his motives.

"Come, a new filly arrived early this mornin'." Larissa stood and grasped Sophronie's hand. "I ken ye'd want to see her."

"I do wish to, of course." She set the novel aside. "Let me fetch a wrap, and I'll meet you in the foyer. It's noticeably cooler today."

"Aye, Evan says we may have an early snow," Larissa said, her eyes glowing with anticipation. "Then there'll be sleddin', skatin', and gallons of hot mulled wine and cider."

An early snow would hamper Sophronie's newly devised plans to leave without the annulment she sought.

Five minutes later, Sophronie descended the wide staircase. She'd skipped a bonnet and chosen to wear a simple navy-blue woolen cloak. It had been among her clothing that had arrived from London several weeks ago.

As she walked down the corridor to the foyer, voices stretched from the entrance to her. Not only was Larissa waiting for her bundled in a thick cloak, but so were Sarah and Rosalind.

"We wanted to see the filly too," Sarah said, tying her bonnet beneath her chin. Her eyes held a mischievous gleam. "We promise to be quiet, so the mother doesna become nervous."

There was something magical about seeing a newborn foal—anything newborn for that matter. It was as close to a miracle as the average person would ever get, and Sophronie never ceased to be awed at the Almighty's handiwork.

As they trekked the pathway to the stables, the women chatted gaily. The autumn wind whipped at the hems of their skirts, and the cold nipped their cheeks and noses. Laughing, they entered the warm stables, and Sophronie inhaled deeply.

She adored the smell of horses and hay.

To her surprise, Anna, the grandmothers, and the aunts, as she'd come to think of them, were also in the barn. She supposed everyone was excited to see the newest addition to Evan's stables.

"Sophronie."

She turned upon hearing Evan's voice behind her, and her heart stopped before resuming beating with a frenzy.

That was no filly.

"*Cinnamon*," she choked, barely able to say her beloved mare's name.

Muscular legs braced, he stood there, hair tousled from the wind and an enigmatic smile upon his lips.

"Cinnamon," Sophronie said again, unable to believe her eyes.

Cinnamon neighed, lifting her head up and down in excitement and scraping the ground with her hoof.

Tears streaming down her cheeks, Sophronie ran to the mare and threw her arms around her neck.

"I've missed you so, so much," she sobbed into the horse's warm hide.

Laughter and clapping broke out behind her, and she realized Evan's entire family had been in on the surprise. They were truly special people, and she'd come to love them these past weeks.

Cinnamon bent and wrapped her neck around Sophronie, hugging her back.

"Would ye look at that," Brody McFarland said in amazement. "Never in all of my years have I seen a horse hug a human."

"It takes a special bond," Evan said in an unexpectedly gravelly voice somewhere near her ear. "Verra few people are ever as privileged, and those who are have a rare affinity for horseflesh. Sophronie is one of those unique people."

The emotion and admiration in his tenor brought another swell of tears to her eyes. Coming from him, it was great praise indeed.

She glanced up, meeting his eyes, and her breath hitched at the smoldering emotion she saw in those blue-gray depths. It made her hot all over and heavy in her belly. Her feet moved toward him of their own volition, and she hugged him tightly.

"Thank you, Evan. Thank you."

He encircled her with his strong arms, and she never wanted him to stop holding her. It felt so right. So natural.

"I'd do anything to bring a smile to yer face, *leannan*."

She leaned back, searching his gentle eyes. She could've loved this man in another time and place. Would've done anything to win his heart, but that option was stolen from her.

"Anything?"

He kissed her forehead with such reverent tenderness, tears sprang to her eyes. "Anythin' but let ye go."

18

Evan gazed into his wife's teary eyes, full of gratitude and joy, and his heart swelled with such love, his ribs ached. This petite firebrand with streaks of fire and sun in her hair, who was frequently in a tangle of some sort and often went against Society's expectations and strictures, had wiggled her way into his heart.

By God, he was fiercely glad for it. Ferociously thankful that circumstances had brought her into his life and made her his wife. No other woman challenged him to be a better person, forced him to examine himself, caused him to realize what was truly important in the scheme of life like Sophronie, his darling unconventional duchess, had done.

Yes, they'd grated on each other. Rubbed one

another raw at times.

Regardless, that sparking of flint against steel had ignited a passion and love of profound strength and endurance. Nothing he'd ever before experienced with another woman or could ever experience in the future could compare.

Sophronie was splendidly unique, gloriously exceptional, and in every way made him a better person. Evan didn't care that she was an American, or that she wasn't an aristocrat, or that she said or did things *le beau monde* took exception to.

She made him complete.

They fit together—even if her hurt, sorrow, and sense of betrayal didn't allow her to see that yet. Evan must persist until he broke through her self-erected barriers, and she was able to, at last, recognize the truth.

They were always meant to be together. It was their destiny.

By divine providence and grace, he'd been gifted this marvelous woman as his wife. Only a simple-minded, selfish imbecile would reject such an unexpected and treasured blessing.

Sophronie believed the only reason he refused to grant her an annulment was because he was obstinate and wanted to gain control of her half of the fortune.

In point of fact, he didn't want to face a future without her. Convincing her of that would take some doing, but he was a patient man. Still, she needed to remain in residence for him to persuade her how much she'd come to mean to him.

"We'll see ye in the house, Evan," his mother called, pulling her fur-lined mantle closer about her shoulders. "Dinna be late for luncheon. We have guests coming and a special birthday to celebrate."

"We willna be overly long, Mother."

Amid smiles, teasing, and a few speculative glances, his female relatives departed the barn. The stable hands went about their chores, leaving Evan and Sophronie alone.

"She's a bonnie lass." Evan ran his hand down the mare's withers. "How old is she?"

"She's eight." Pride shone in Sophronie's eyes as she stroked the horse. "I halter trained and broke her myself, though it didn't take much doing. She was born at Woodmead Hill and had seen so many other horses being ridden, she took to it as naturally as a duck to water."

Evan smoothed a strand of fly-away hair over her delicate ear. "Sophronie, I vow ye are the most extraordinary woman I've ever met."

A smile blossomed across her radiant face, and his heart sang. Her happiness made him content, and her sorrow grieved his spirit.

A barn cat exited one of the stalls and jumped up on a bale of hay. She sat upon her haunches and proceeded to groom her mottled gray fur. Outside, rooks called to one another, their raucous caws strident in the morning's foggy calm.

It was a gloomy day by anyone's standards, yet never had Evan felt as optimistic and light-hearted as he did at this moment.

"Would ye like to go for a ride?"

"Oh, yes, and I'm sure Cinnamon would too after her ocean voyage." Something akin to affection made her azure eyes even brighter. "Just give me a few minutes to change into a riding habit."

No, she couldn't leave. This harmony between them was too precious. Something had changed. Evan felt it in his spirit.

"Canna ye ride her astride in what ye have on?" He flicked her cloak, profoundly reluctant to let her go with this fragile new intimacy sparking between them.

"I can." Sophronie pressed a kiss to Cinnamon's neck. She kept her gaze averted, her profile to him. "But I thought you preferred that I behave with more decorum fitting a woman of my new station."

A Highlander's boot to Evan's breastbone would've hurt less than those words.

That she would try to change to become what she thought were his perceptions of a lady exhilarated him and simultaneously cleaved his soul in two. Sophronie was wrong. He didn't want to change a damn thing about her. She was perfection just as she was, and he'd been a blind fool not to have seen it before.

"I don't want my actions to bring censure on the duchy." She closed her eyes and pressed her cheek against Cinnamon's neck, as if she couldn't bear to see Evan's censure and disapproval.

Evan cursed inwardly.

God rot him for all of the times he'd insinuated she was gauche and unladylike. Though unintentional, he'd made her feel inferior as if she was wanting and deficient because she wasn't afraid to forge her own path. Her independence and intrepidness were qualities he'd come to admire most in her.

"Sophronie, ye are a shinin' light in a gray and gloomy world. That can never bring disgrace upon the dukedom." Love for her deepened his voice to a gravelly tenor. "In fact, I can say with sincerity and awe that there will never be a Duchess of Waycross who compares to ye."

Her mouth softened into a delighted "O," and a blush tinted her smooth cheeks, accenting the faint constellation of gingerish freckles there. "Go on with you. I never took you for the sort to wax poetic."

"I've never been more serious in my life."

Her hair glowed with sunset hues in the muted stable light. A memory of those long tresses hanging to her waist that night he'd encountered her in the library flashed to mind. His fingers itched to comb through that silky mass. To lay her on the carpet before the fireplace and worship her with his mouth and body.

Evan stepped nearer until his thigh touched hers. He cupped her shoulders and rotated her so that she faced him. "Darlin', I want ye to be happy. If that means ridin' astride, or stark naked, then I willna object."

His groin swelled at the sensual image of her naked atop her horse, a gentle breeze playing with her hair, and her pert breasts, high and full, jiggling as she rode.

Ye gods, man. Control yerself.

Slanting her head, Sophronie studied him, reminding him of the curious sparrows that ventured into the barn from time to time to steal a bit of corn or oat. A husky chuckle slipped past her lips. "Not even I am brave enough to ride across the moors without a stitch when the ominous skies portend snow."

Cupping her cheek, he lowered his head.

"I wish to kiss ye, wife."

Her lips parted, and her eyes went round before her attention dipped to his mouth.

"You may."

"*Ye may?*" Laughing, he scooped her into his arms

and nuzzled her creamy neck.

She gave a starchy huff and angled away from him. "Well, a proper lady wouldn't declare she wanted a man to kiss her. Would she?"

"First, I am no' just any man but yer husband." He kissed her nose. "Secondly, ye are nae a proper lady—"

She went rigid in his arms and glared up at him. "Why, of all of the impolite things—"

"Shh." Evan pressed his mouth to hers. "Dinna fash yerself."

He replaced his lips with a finger to her petal-soft lips to keep her silent.

Her blue eyes flashed, but she didn't struggle or curse him to Hades.

"I was goin' to say, I dinna want a proper lady if that means someone who doesna tell me what is on her mind, who is afraid to be herself around me and be wholly honest with me at all times. I much prefer ye, lass. Ye make me laugh, and every day, ye surprise me. Life with ye will never be borin'."

Frowning, she fingered his lapel. "I'm not certain those are compliments."

"Trust me, Roni, they are. I'm no' eloquent with my words, but I am sincere in what I say." He tipped her chin up. "Now hush and let me kiss ye properly."

Cinnamon whickered as if in approval.

Sophronie gave the horse a penetrating look. "She likes you."

"Of course she does. She kens how much I adore her mistress."

"Do you truly, Evan?"

He traced her eyebrow with his fingertip. "I ken ye have reason to doubt me, darlin', but I vow before God and may He strike me dead if I do no' speak the truth. My heart is yers whether ye want it or no'."

19

Still in the Stables

Now three curious barn cats and two more horses are watching

Evan tucked his wife into the crook of his arm and kissed her with all of the passion and hunger he'd kept at bay these past weeks. If he lived to be a hundred, he'd never have enough time with his woman.

He'd realized weeks before that he could not let Sophronie go.

She'd take his soul with him.

Sighing, she melted against him, clutching his coat. She returned the onslaught of his kisses in her typical fashion, exuberant if not particularly skillful. Still, his blood heated, and his groin hardened as he nipped and nibbled his way from her mouth to her ear, down her neck, and lower still.

"Evan," she breathed, her voice raspy. "I feel so odd. Hot and hungry but in a way that is hard to describe. As if there's something more I crave, but I don't know what it is."

Naturally Sophronie, being Sophronie, would have a conversation in the middle of scorching kisses to discuss the new sensations.

"That's passion, my love, and I feel it too." He grazed his mouth along her neck, and she shuddered. "And there is more. Much more."

"I think," she said, her voice sultry with desire, "that I may wish to explore the *more*."

Evan raised his head and stared deep into her passion-drugged eyes. "I'd like nothin' more than to teach ye. But then ye'd be my wife, truly no' just in name. Is that what ye want, lass?"

She looked past his shoulder for a long moment. So long, in fact, he feared she'd changed her mind.

"Is that what *you* want, Evan?" Her eyelashes fluttered downward. "I know I'm not who you would've chosen to be your duchess. If we consummate our vows, will we regret it later on?"

He placed his palms on both sides of her face. "I would have nae other, ever, Sophronie. I shall let ye choose when and if we make our marriage real. But ken this, if ye decide nae, I shall honor my vow and be faithful to ye until I draw my dyin' breath."

~*~

Sophronie's mind warred with her heart as she peered into her husband's eyes. "Are you saying you love me?"

He gave her a playful scowl.

"If ye are unsure after what I just said, lass, then I need to work on my poetic prose."

His expression sobered, and he lifted her hand to his mouth. Pressing a kiss to her wrist where her pulse beat a fervent staccato, he gave her such a smoldering look through half-closed lids, her knees actually shook.

"Aye, duchess wife." His voice grew husky with emotion. "I love ye. I love ye so verra much, I canna express with mere words."

Joy thrummed through Sophronie.

Evan loved her. He really loved her. The misfit hoyden from America.

"I didn't know how to win your heart, Evan, after everything we'd been through."

"*Leannan,* ye won this duke's heart long before I recognized I'd given it to you. We're like those horses we raise, I think. Fighting the halter, bit, saddle, and rider until we stopped resisting and realized we were the better for it."

Nothing else mattered. Not that Evan and Sophronie had been at odds from the moment they'd met. Not that theirs had been a marriage of convenience. Not all of the misunderstandings and harsh words between them.

Evan loved her.

And Sophronie loved him.

That was the unidentifiable feeling that had flummoxed and bewildered her these many weeks. She didn't recognize her love because resentment and distrust had blinded her to the beautiful, unexpected truth.

She loved Evan.

Putting her palm to his cheek, she raised up on tip toes.

"I love you too, Evan. I do. It scares me how much because I don't think I can be the type of wife you need. The sort of wife the duchy deserves."

With an elated whoop, Evan wrapped her in his embrace.

"Yer love is enough, darlin'. It has always been and will always be sufficient."

His mouth claimed hers in a demanding, heated kiss, and Sophronie responded with the love she'd finally allowed herself to acknowledge. It was heady and intoxicating and made her giddy.

His breathing ragged, Evan raised his head. "I have somethin' for yer birthday." He fished inside his coat pocket for a few seconds then withdrew a ring. He held it up between his thumb and forefinger.

A half hoop scrolled and carved gold band interlaid with three sapphires and two diamonds sparkled up at her.

"I never asked ye to be my wife, Sophronie, but I

am askin' ye now. Can ye put our past behind us and forge a future with me? I want ye to be the first thing I see when I wake each morn and the last when I close my eyes at night."

"Yes, Evan. That is what I want too." She truly did with all of her heart. Tears blurred her eyes, but Sophronie blinked them away. "I want to bear your children and share every aspect of my life with you. "

She held her hand out, and giving her a wicked grin, he slid the ring on. He nuzzled her neck, and she giggled.

"I say, lady duchess, what if we take a different sort of ride this mornin'?"

He gave her a rakish wink, and heat skated up Sophronie's cheeks.

"What did you have in mind?" she teased, knowing full well what he meant.

"Come with me, and I'll show ye." Evan waggled his eyebrows. "Ye willna need a ridin' habit either."

Sophronie laughed, the pure unadulterated laugh of one who has found their soul mate. Who had given their trust and future to another without a qualm. "How can I resist so romantic an invitation?"

"Ye canna, because I am as temptin' to ye as ye are to me." He led Cinnamon into a stall and secured the door. Masculine confidence in every step, he strode back to Sophronie and extended his hand.

How could a person's heart be this overflowing and not burst?

She slipped her hand in his, and it was as if she'd finally come home after a long, lonely absence. "It is true. I would be your wife in every way, Evan."

Laughing, they turned and ran to face their future. Together.

Epilogue

Mayfair, London, England
May 1811—morning

Resting his head on his elbow, Evan trailed a finger over his sleeping wife's ivory shoulder. She stirred but didn't wake. As was typical, he'd awakened with a raging cockstand, but his pregnant wife needed her rest. So, despite the angry member throbbing between his legs, he contented himself with feathering touches on velvety skin as she slept on.

His exploration of her silky flesh took him lower until he skimmed his fingertips over the lush contour of her hip and slipped behind her knee.

She giggled and swatted at his inquisitive hand. "Stop that, you rogue. I'm sleeping."

Chuckling, Evan flipped her over, pinning her to the mattress.

Still groggy, Sophronie smiled up at him then yawned.

"You're awake early, Evan. What time is it?"

She tried to turn her head to see the clock on the nightstand.

"Time for me to show my lady duchess how much I love her." He ran his tongue over the delicate shell of her ear and was gratified to feel her shudder beneath him. Sophronie was as uninhibited and daring between the sheets as she was in every other aspect of her life.

"I think, my lord husband, that will soon be obvious for all to see." Pointing her attention between their bodies, she lovingly caressed the slight mound of her belly.

Evan grinned and flexed his hips against hers. "I'm as proud as any man who ever breathed for the world to ken ye will bear my child." He placed his palm atop Sophronie's much smaller hand. He kissed her tummy. "Good mornin', bairn."

"I was positive I wouldn't mind being pregnant for

the Season, but now I'm not certain. The Duchesses of Bainbridge, Asherford, and Westfall have chosen to abstain from the Season, and I am further along than they are. I do want the babe born at Balston House with our family."

The current high waistline in women's gowns hid Sophronie's condition from all but the most discerning. Braced on his elbows, Evan studied his wife's face. He knew her better than himself, and the wee furrow between her eyebrows gave her away. "Did something happen at the ball last night?"

She glanced to the side, then puffed out a little frustrated breath. "I ran into Leah Wesleyan in the ladies' retiring room."

"I dinna ken she'd be there." Evan grunted and flopped onto his back, one hand across his waist and the other above his head. "I dinna think to ask the host beforehand."

Sophronie lifted a shoulder as she placed both hands upon her stomach. "If we come up to London, it's inevitable that we'll run into her from time to time."

"What did she do?" Evan had no doubt the bitter

233

hell-cat had bared her claws. He should've told her to leave the continent, or he'd make known her crimes.

"Let's just say she's not forgiven either of us, and I found myself fearing for our child should she learn I am pregnant." She gave Evan a sidelong look. "I know it's silly."

Not after what Leah had done to George Slater, it wasn't.

He made a mental note to change his plans for the day. He would call on Leah Wesleyan and suggest she would be better served in Paris or Rome or Timbuktu. Anywhere but England or Scotland. He'd give her a week to make herself scarce.

"We can return to Scotland today if ye wish, sweetheart." Evan drew Sophronie against him and cradled her head upon his shoulder. Running his fingers through her hair as he'd imagined doing all of those months ago, he said, "My man of business can handle most everythin' for me."

Sophronie wrapped an arm about his naked waist and laid a slender thigh across both of his. "No." She shook her head. "I'm not running away ever again. I'd rather stay and face my fears."

All the more reason to see Leah Wesleyan out of the country.

"That's my brave, bonnie lass." Evan kissed her tenderly.

Her enthusiastic response caused the ember he'd kept in check to ignite, and within seconds he was deep inside her woman's warmth. As he rocked into her, relishing her whimpers and moans, he whispered words of love and passion into her ear or rained hot kisses over any bare flesh he could reach with his mouth.

"Ev-an!" Clutching his shoulders, Sophronie went taut and found her release.

His followed a half-second later.

As he smoothed her damp hair from her forehead, he thanked God again for this woman. "I love ye, Roni."

Expression contemplative, she linked her fingers with his.

"My father was right about us."

"George Slater was a wise man." Evan kissed her temple.

"If you'd let me have my way about an annulment,

we'd never have known this happiness." Sophronie gave him a smile that melted his once-hardened heart. "I cannot promise not to be mulish and obstinate in the future. I'm afraid it's my nature."

Evan gathered her hand in his and kissed each fingertip. "I'm countin' on it. I like the makin' up afterward a great deal."

"As do I." She giggled. "Perhaps I shall deliberately provoke you."

"Wanton wench," he murmured, sliding her atop him and slipping home. "What am I to do with ye?"

"What you are doing right now will suffice very nicely," she said between gasps of pleasure.

Then words fled them as Evan took them to heaven's gates once more.

About the Author

USA Today Bestselling, award-winning author COLLETTE CAMERON® scribbles Scottish and Regency historicals featuring dashing rogues and scoundrels and the intrepid damsels who reform them. Blessed with an overactive and witty muse that won't stop whispering new romantic romps in her ear, she's lived in Oregon her entire life, though she dreams of living in Scotland part-time. A self-confessed Cadbury chocoholic, you'll always find a dash of inspiration and a pinch of humor in her sweet-to-spicy timeless romances®.

Explore **Collette's worlds** at
collettecameron.com!

Join her **VIP Reader Club** and **FREE newsletter**.
Giggles guaranteed!

FREE BOOK: Join Collette's The Regency Rose®
VIP Reader Club to get updates on book releases, cover
reveals, contests, and giveaways she reserves
exclusively for email and newsletter followers. Also,
any deals, sales, or special promotions are offered to
club members first. She will not share your name or
email, nor will she spam you.

http://bit.ly/TheRegencyRoseGift

Follow Collette on BookBub
www.bookbub.com/authors/collette-cameron

From the Desk of Collette Cameron

Thank you for reading HOW TO WIN A DUKE'S HEART. I hope you've enjoyed the latest installment in my SEDUCTIVE SCOUNDRELS SERIES.

For centuries, horse racing was a popular sport in Britain and Scotland. The Ayr Gold Cup, known as the Western Meeting from 1824 onward, did in fact, take place in Ayr, Scotland. Although the race usually took place in September, I also found August (1804) and October dates. For the benefit of my storyline and because the race had only been occurring for a few years by 1810, I chose an August date. I also chose a Tuesday because the few specific dates I could find for the race in the early 1800s were on Tuesdays.

The races at Ayr were supported by the landed gentry and local nobility in the area. I couldn't find an exact prize purse for the 1810 race, so I settled on 1000 pounds which was half of the prize money awarded for the 1824 race. £1000 was a veritable fortune in those days. I took a bit of creative liberty and mentioned prizes for winners of privately sponsored competitions too.

I also took artistic liberty in having a duke marry a commoner. That trope pops up often in rags to riches or Cinderella-themed stories. It would've been frowned upon and could've caused quite a scandal, but a duke would not lose his title over such a choice.

To ensure you don't miss it, subscribe to The Regency Rose, my newsletter (Get a free book too!). I also have a fabulous VIP Reader Group on Facebook. If you're a fan of my books and historical romance, I'd love to have you join me. You'll also be the first to see new covers, read exclusive excerpts, be the first to know about contests and giveaways, help me pick titles and name characters, and much, much more!

If you'd like to learn a bit more about the other characters mentioned in HOW TO WIN A DUKE'S HEART, here are their books.

Tobias Forsythe, Duke of Heatherston: WHEN A DUKE DESIRES A LASS—the next book in the Seductive Scoundrels series.

Nicolette Pembroke, Duchess of Westfall: NEVER

DANCE WITH A DUKE

Ophelia Bancroft, Duchess of Asherford: LOVED BY A DANGEROUS DUKE

Jessica Rolston, Duchess of Bainbridge: WOOED BY A WICKED DUKE.

Baxter Bathhurst, Duke of San Sebastian: WEDDING HER CHRISTMAS DUKE

Please consider telling other readers why you enjoyed this book by reviewing it. I also truly adore hearing from my readers. You can contact me on my website and, while you are there, explore my author world. If you enjoyed reading Evan and Sophronie's story, be sure to check out the other books in my SEDUCTIVE SCOUNDRELS SERIES.

Hugs,

Collette

A Diamond for a Duke

Seductive Scoundrels, Book One

A dour duke. A wistful wallflower.
An impossible match.

Jules, Sixth Duke of Dandridge disdains Society and all its trappings, preferring the country's solitude and peace. Already jaded after the woman he loved died years ago, he's become even more so since unexpectedly inheriting a dukedom's responsibilities and finding himself the target of every husband-hunting vixen and matchmaker mother in London.

Jemmah Dament has adored Jules from afar for years—since before her family's financial and social reversals. She dares not dream she can win a duke's heart any more than she hopes to escape the life of servitude imposed on her by an uncaring mother. Jemmah knows full well Jules is too far above her station now. Besides, his family has already selected his perfect duchess: a poised, polished, exquisite blueblood.

chance encounter reunites Jules and Jemmah, resulting in a passionate interlude neither can forget. Jules realizes he wants more—much more—than Jemmah's sweet kisses or her warming his bed. He must somehow convince her to gamble on a dour duke. But can Jemmah trust a man promised to another? One who's sworn never to love again?